Praise for *The Yellow Kitchen*:

'Rich and thoroughly intoxicating, *The Yellow Kitchen* is a sensual journey into friendship, food and female sexuality, full of complex, fascinating characters and bold ideas. I loved it'
Rosie Walsh, author of *The Love of My Life*

'A heady mix of politics, friendship, sex and food, poignant, provocative and utterly distinctive'
Paula Hawkins, author of *The Girl on the Train*

'An exquisite novel – beautifully rendered, powerfully told, and so deeply felt. I urge you to read this novel – you will never forget it'
Lucia Osborne-Crowley, author of
My Body Keeps Your Secrets

'Mixing female friendship, romance, loss, redemption, and memorable meals, *The Yellow Kitchen* is the perfect recipe for a flavourful literary feast. With subtle dashes of wit and generous sprinklings of honesty, Margaux Vialleron has crafted a brave and tender tale'   **Kim Fay, author of *Love & Saffron***

'*The Yellow Kitchen* is so warm and convivial in atmosphere, and its discussion of the politics of the UK and their impact very poignant. It portrayed beautifully the sense of adventure of being a certain age, with its rush and richness and emotional confusion, and I found it such a satisfying read'
Emily Itami, author of *Fault Lines*

'Stylishly written, this witty portrayal of the appetites and private passions of a young group of friends is a moreish and utterly satisfying feast, best devoured slowly over a few delicious sittings' **Caroline Eden, author of *Red Sands***

'Set in 2019, at a time of intense political change in the UK, this is a rich novel that explores the complexities of female friendship and sexuality, love and politics' ***Daily Mail***

'Vialleron's debut weaves the complexities of female friend-ships in with attractions, desire, politics and food' ***Stylist***

The
Yellow
Kitchen

Margaux
Vialleron

**SIMON &
SCHUSTER**

London · New York · Sydney · Toronto · New Delhi

First published in Great Britain by Simon & Schuster UK Ltd, 2022
This paperback edition published in 2023

Copyright © Margaux Vialleron, 2022

The right of Margaux Vialleron to be identified as
author of this work has been asserted in accordance
with the Copyright, Designs and Patents Act, 1988.

1 3 5 7 9 10 8 6 4 2

Simon & Schuster UK Ltd
1st Floor
222 Gray's Inn Road
London WC1X 8HB

Simon & Schuster Australia,
Sydney

Simon & Schuster India,
New Delhi

www.simonandschuster.co.uk
www.simonandschuster.com.au
www.simonandschuster.co.in

Annie Ernaux, excerpt from *A Frozen Woman*, translated by
Linda Coverdale. Copyright © 1981 by Éditions Gallimard. Translation
copyright © 1995 by Seven Stories Press. Reprinted with the permission
of The Permissions Company, LLC on behalf of Seven Stories Press,
sevenstories.com.

The author and publishers have made all reasonable efforts to contact
copyright-holders for permission, and apologise for any omissions or errors
in the form of credits given. Corrections may be made to future printings.

A CIP catalogue record for this book is available from the British Library

Paperback ISBN: 978-1-3985-0849-1
eBook ISBN: 978-1-3985-0848-4
Audio ISBN: 978-1-3985-1354-9

This book is a work of fiction. Names, characters, places and incidents
are either a product of the author's imagination or are used fictitiously.
Any resemblance to actual people living or dead, events or locales
is entirely coincidental.

Typeset in Bembo by
Palimpsest Book Production Ltd, Falkirk, Stirlingshire
Printed and Bound in the UK using 100% Renewable Electricity
at CPI Group (UK) Ltd

MIX
Paper | Supporting
responsible forestry
FSC
www.fsc.org   FSC® C171272

Pour Maman

She teaches me that the world is made to be pounced on and enjoyed, and that there is absolutely no reason at all to hold back.

Annie Ernaux, *A Frozen Woman*, 1995

Few days are remembered as exceptional. History books weigh heavy on schoolchildren's backs, photo albums gather dust inside drawers, diaries fill up with events and deadlines, the watches we tighten onto our wrists, the time-trackers of our hunt for the next date to remember. London, E17, fewer hours than days left until the year of 2019 begins, a kitchen with yellow walls holds three friends together. Claude, Giulia and Sophie.

Claude stares expectantly at the kitchen counter, where olive pits, baking trays and pools of oil clutter the surface. 'Béchamel is all about patience,' she declares.

'Like most things in life,' adds Sophie, the popping sound of a cork punctuating the rhythm of her voice. Pinot Noir, a compact beverage that matches the heavy sky over North London, its colour overwhelmingly lilac like clouds on the cusp of snow.

Claude slowly and delicately begins to pour milk into a saucepan, one serving spoon at a time, while Giulia is stirring the béchamel robustly from the opposite end of the hob. She responds after a short silence: 'That's a shame. I have little patience left in me.'

The creamy sauce comes to a soft boil and Claude lowers the heat, a thickening cloud forming between them as the evening embraces the room. Lights switch on, the smell of milk and butter highlights the bitter taste of the wine, the women's bones whirl stone-cold as the wind blows through the thin kitchen window. They warmed up the milk before pouring the liquid into the sauce, that is the trick. The secret their grandmothers and mothers gifted them, each experienced through different home countries, cultures that are on the edge of a break-up; the EU withdrawal agreement under negotiation, a sentence due to fall this upcoming year, the scribbled recipes the previous generations abandon once there is no flesh left for them to feed. Tonight, the three friends agree to warm up the milk in a saucepan first, melt butter and flour in a separate pot, a grind of nutmeg for Giulia, a bay leaf for Sophie and a pinch of salt for Claude. That is the trick for a good béchamel, they agree.

The kitchen is narrow but this is the room where the memory of their friendship is enclosed. A yellowing shell, like coral resting on sand at the bottom of the ocean, a once-upon-a-time shining pearl safely hiding inside. They painted the walls in a vivid mustard yellow, 'like the kitchen of Marguerite

Duras.' Giulia and Sophie did not dare ask further questions; it is Claude's home, after all. She still hasn't got round to refurbishing the old-fashioned black-and-white tile flooring. They'd grown to like it, ever since the night Giulia turned up at the flat with a bottle of Cono Sur Bicicleta Pinot Noir, a wine renowned for its reliable stock levels across London's neighbourhoods and corner shops. She was on her way back from her latest dispiriting date, another spate of daily texting that had failed to deliver the stimulating face-to-face conversations she had rehearsed for. Sophie was already there and a few drinks in, avoiding meeting Giulia's eyes for the first half an hour, making her work for a truce after she had intruded on Sophie's night with Claude in the yellow kitchen. A bitter appetiser until they found each other as a trio again, on the floor, playing a game of checkers with empty bottles. Claude's yellow kitchen and dreams of making a living from her baking, Sophie's career ambitions and glorious relationship, Giulia's activism and disappointing dating life hanging between them, discords in the search for a contented middle ground. They cherish such a childish but shared memory of a time together so tightly, they cannot possibly change the flooring. The yellow kitchen is where they reunite to commemorate each one of their life events, however small, joyful, raging or sad. The wobbly, dark oak cupboards do not close properly after years of being slammed. There is a small, solar-powered radio on the counter, and no one is allowed to touch it since Giulia found the best station. They don't know which frequency the radio is set to, however the sun makes rare appearances in that corner of the kitchen and thus the music is mostly silent. They drink wine from old chipped cups, spending long nights debating why the shelves in the cupboards are not spaced far enough apart to accommodate wine glasses. Is the owner a recovering alcoholic? Do they intend to remind them of their place in society? *No wine glasses for you, girls.* Who owns the yellow kitchen? Are they even aware that wine glasses do not fit in the cupboards?

31 December 2018, Claude, Giulia and Sophie are layering sheets of pasta in the form of a lasagna for a shared meal. The timer ticks as the room warms. Sophie turns on the oven before stepping back; Claude and Giulia move around the kitchen, peeling and slicing mushrooms. When Giulia begins to grate parmesan and slice mozzarella, Sophie turns towards Claude to ask her about the yellow vest movements in France. Claude continues to stir the vegetables in a frying pan, a tear conjured by the smell of whitening onions, her gaze focused until she taps the wooden spoon aside and she twirls to face Sophie.

'I know very little about the yellow vests.' She pauses. 'Would you like to start layering pasta sheets at the bottom of the oven dish?'

Sophie executes, topping up her drink on the way. Claude allows herself a soft cough, then she reminds her friends she has not travelled to France for a long time. She refuses to be the spokesperson for the country and its politics among them simply because of her name, the dreaded rhythm of double vowels followed by their reciprocal consonant. Claude. Giulia brings in the cheese and they start working around the oven dish together: a third of the béchamel, a third of the vegetables and a third of cheese. They repeat the same layering method twice, their hands labour in concert, empowered with Giulia's energy as she makes a plea in defence for the yellow vests. She reports that groups are gathering together throughout the world, small pockets of hope made of real people.

'This is not only about petrol or commodity prices. No.' Her voice rises above the backdrop of the tired oven fan. 'It's a wave of people who have had enough. They want to work towards something tangible, like a roof or a meal to share, and not against a system. I think it's beautiful, however disruptive they may be.'

Sophie returns to the bowl of grated parmesan and adds extra on top of the final layer, a shy but meaningful smile breaks her lips as she draws the lasagna to a close. Claude opens the oven's door and sets the timer. The smell of béchamel and cheese comes in waves through the yellow kitchen as they toast the coming new year.

When they finally sit at the table, plates steaming before them, Giulia must remind them she has never had a white lasagna before, her tastebuds sharp and earthy, the child of ragù Bolognese. Claude and Sophie nod back at Giulia, their expressions tender but tight. Sophie wanted to add asparagus, longing for summertime. The radio is miraculously working tonight, a special New Year's Eve show runs in the background as clocks rapidly approach the midnight high tide, promised celebrations looming. Forks and knives in hands, the three women cut through the pasta; the béchamel sauce and gummy mushrooms appear in a cloud, the first bite loosens their tongues. Claude turns down the radio so they can hear each other.

On the first day of January 2019, the expectations of a new year shadow the disappointments from the previous four seasons. Claude, Giulia and Sophie are consuming life, determined to be grown-ups.

Claude

Our kitchen when I was a child was milky white, long as a
corridor and compact like a spiderweb. The left wall was
covered with fast-slamming cupboards and the right side
accommodated a bar with one stool only. I ate all my meals
sitting on this chair for a throne, challenging my balance,
learning to sit straight and strong, while Maman leant on
the kitchen counter, staring at walls greying from simmering
ratatouille and draining steamy water from pasta.

I had never seen the light inside the oven switched on until
the week of my first-ever birthday outing. May 1999, I was
seven years old. I brought a flashy blue envelope back from
school, *Claude* written on the front in cursive and careful
letters, meticulously flattened between two exercise books
in my cartable so it would not crumple. I left it on the
coffee table before bed for Maman to find it later in the
night.

The next day, she woke me up early enough to go to the supermarket before school. I remember how fast my feet moved as we entered this bright grotto, full of signs and noises and smells. My senses became hyper-stimulated. I was awake. Supermarkets introduced me to new words, letters I had never seen together before and colours I had only met in my pencil case, flavours I longed to make my own. Maman walked with the same assured pace with which she dressed herself each time we came downstairs from our apartment on the sixth floor of a cement block building, our steps echoing through the unpainted stairwell, bouncing off the fading red guardrail. As soon as the supermarket's sliding doors opened, she seized the sleeve of my jacket, decisively walking towards the baking aisle, undistracted by the yellow promotion signs, not slowing down as an elderly woman's voice rose from the speakers to announce further discounts. Before I had time to count all the way to one hundred, we were back outside, lightheaded from the sudden change in lighting and drop in decibels, a box of Betty Crocker Zesty Lemon Cake Mix and six eggs in our hands. *Simply add eggs, oil, water and icing*, the package read.

When I came back from school that afternoon, I found the cake preparation and eggs abandoned on the kitchen counter. I sat and began to read the back of the package attentively, and I read it again, as many times as it took before Maman re-entered our home:

8

The Yellow Kitchen

*Sugar, Wheat Flour, Palm Fat, Raising Agents: Sodium
Bicarbonate, Monocalcium Phosphate, Modified Corn Starch, Corn
Starch, Emulsifiers: Propane-1, 2-Diol Esters of Fatty Acids,
Mono- and Diglycerides of Fatty Acids, Sodium Stearoyl-2-
Lactylate, Flavouring, Dextrose, Salt, Stabiliser: Xanthan Gum,
Colour: B-Carotene, Acidity Regulator: Citric Acid*

May contain Milk, Egg and Soy traces

I read all these words out loud, meticulously enunciating each syllable, repeating and wondering what they were, what form, feel and smell they inhabited in the world. I wished we owned a dictionary like the one we shared in our classroom, so I could better understand the words that make for a birthday cake. Maman came back, turned the oven on to 180°C fan, grabbed a bowl and a fork and handed them to me. She nodded, 'Allez Claude, c'est ton gâteau,' she passed the scissors. I cut, slowly and in a straight line as they taught me in school, and pushed the yellow mixture through into the bowl. Stodgy and bubbly, the batter dripped at a snail's pace. I cracked the two eggs open, picked out leftover shells with my fingers, poured in water and oil. I mixed everything together with the fork, inhaling the sweetness resulting from the movement of my hands, encouraging me to increase my pace. Maman took the bowl away from me, poured the mixture into a cake tin and slid it into the oven. I did not move for the next twenty minutes, the timer running in one sticky hand – *tic tac tic tac tic tac* – sucking my other thumb.

It came out bright and moist, our achievement in the form of a lemon cake. I gently carried the cake all the way to my friend's home, proudly displaying it among the other goods on the table, colourful napkins and confetti lying around. The day unfolded with games of Twister and hide-and-seek, the children snatching slices of the red velvet layered cake, the chocolate brownies, the vanilla cupcakes – these children's dreams of homemade baked goods – as they ran past the table. Apart from the one slice I had eaten, my Betty Crocker Zesty Lemon cake stood untouched, in the absence of a homemade glaze but featuring granulated, repulsive industrial citrus spikes. When I walked home, quiet tears ran down my cheeks and I promised my little self that the next time I served a cake, I would know for certain if it contained milk, eggs and soy. I told Maman I won the round of Sleeping Lions and I made new friends. I omitted to mention the left-behind cake. She looked at me with proud eyes.

Itchy eyes, achy body awakening from a feverish nightmare the following night, I found Maman sitting on the sofa in the living room, which also made for her bedroom, knitting a jumper in front of a bowl of plain cornflakes and a touch of milk. The reliable mother, ever awake in the middle of the night. On worrisome nights, she also had a cup of coffee, no milk nor sugar, only the sour liquid between us, like fluids from our unnamed ancestors. I have never seen photos: our apartment had plain white walls throughout. Maman refused to sleep, guarding our house, and yet the bad dreams still reached me. She grew paler, frailer and knitted for longer hours – the *tac tac tic tac tic tac tac* flowing through the needles and echoing as she worked, broken nails and skin drying at the tip of her fingers. The little scratching noise her spoon made as she dug for the last sip of milk, final sweetness of the night. Even when days broke into spring weather, she continued to knit jumpers: Maman is always cold.

On Sundays we bathed. We ran a long bath, squeezed all the leftover soaps from the ending week together, whizzed our hands through the water making bubbles, shy laughter emerging from my tiny body and a nodding smile shaping on my mother's face. I hopped over and into the foaming bathtub; a welcoming warm lagoon for me and then a cold puddle for Maman. She sat on the ice-cold tiles, topless, her hair roughly held up with a clasp, and read Jack London's *The Call of the Wild* to me as I submerged myself in water. She never missed a Sunday. Dimanche soir was the one moment when the world would turn around us as we granted ourselves intimacy: wet hair curling down our backs, her tits hardening, my freckles melting into the redness of my body after meeting with hot water, and Maman's blue lips afterwards. Our memories, a family album in the making.

It was then that I noticed the different shades on her body: bags under her eyes and bruises inside her forearms. Bruises from the long work shifts; bags under her eyes as a result of the food in the fridge that eventually got eaten and the bills that accumulated on the wooden desk in the entrance, and me, petite Claude. Maman was alone, responsible for my aliveness; there was no rest left for her, only worrisome nights, knitting me woollen armour.

Now she has retreated, with sleepy eyes and few words left for her battles, and I move on, instincts alert, expectations high, the call of the wild. *He was mastered by the sheer surging of life, the tidal wave of being, the perfect joy of each separate muscle, joint, and sinew in that it was everything that was not death, that it was aglow and rampant, expressing itself in movement, flying exultantly under the stars and over the face of dead matter that did not move.* I often hear her small whispers in my ears, as my hands meet with flour, butter and eggs, as I whisk.

Spring

1

2019, on a bus. Claude, Sophie and Giulia are sitting in the front row – Claude and Sophie on the left, Giulia on the right, an empty seat next to her. They are wrapped up and agitated, shouting loudly, grabbing each other's arms, tapping their feet against the deck. The weather is grey and chilly outside, but the end of March is fast approaching. Hundreds of thousands are expected to walk through central London this afternoon, in a bid to stop Brexit. They make their way to 10 Downing Street with one goal: to gain a second people's vote, together. It is fair to say they have not always aligned politically – Claude often rolling her eyes at Sophie's liberal discourse; Giulia distributing tracts for the Labour Party – but Brexit is one trauma they share. The hangover they experienced on 24 June 2016. None of them has had a toss of tequila since. Today there is a renewed energy. They met at

Claude's earlier in the morning to have breakfast, the most problematic meal to share since Giulia craves buttery pastries, Claude dreams of egg and soldiers before they march for their rights and Sophie just wants to nibble the crust from the bread. They argued briefly before they agreed on a loaf of bread, butter, either jam or cheese to pick for a topping, and black coffee brewed on a low flame, as they painted signs:

BOLLOCKS TO BREXIT

FROMAGE NOT FARAGE

THE ONLY SINGLE MARKET
I WANT TO LEAVE IS BUMBLE

'Did you know that until 1993 the list of those who had not voted was displayed in the municipal registers in Italy? A *did not vote* note also appeared on certificates of good conduct,' Claude says, after a silence that felt longer than it lasted.

'That's how I feel about my Twitter feed these days,' says Sophie.

'I wish I had a dog so everyone would know that I did go to vote.' There is a further silence before Giulia continues, 'How do you know about this?'

'About?'

'About the registers in Italy,' she clarifies with a hint of annoyance in her voice.

'I read about it at an exhibition in Rome.'

Giulia contemplates adding that she has never been to Rome herself. The sharp and ambient cold, the low winter sky and the blooming expectations of spring make her fierce. She wants to remind her London friends that this so-called race against Brexit is not about securing their rights to travel smoothly for holidays, but about the lives that are held together by the European Union, the dreams and connections that are now drifting, filled with uncertainties, a future flooded with lies. The Erasmus programme that allows students to move around Europe, even when they have not travelled in their own country before; the funds that energise and protect research, agriculture, access to medicines, global security; the social and labour laws that are debated and reviewed at a larger scale, so they can be for the many; the European identity. Giulia came to London soon after she graduated from her History degree, with a specialisation in Culture and Media Communication, from the Università di Bologna. Most of her friends had moved places already and she dreamt of working for a famous London music venue. She does not, she *manages projects*. Giulia's work vaguely relates to marketing and hides a ton of administrative tasks that give her little perspective, but she remains proud that she always knows which song to play next at a party. She even made a playlist for their breakfast this morning, the lyrics that pulse through the politics of their lives.

The three friends don't speak further until they exit the bus. Their bones feel stiff from the pressing state of anxiety.

But they soon warm up, carried away by the crowd in a hurry to find some of their university friends who have joined the streets too. These are the people they reunite with for special occasions and life milestones. Claude and Sophie met them on the floor of their student accommodation, south of the Thames, while Giulia was introduced later, north of the river this time. Their ambitions abruptly moved their daily lives to the heart of the city after they graduated, open-plan office floors securing most of them a premium view over the London skyline and its scaffolds. They chased their careers in progress during the day; their desire for social connection escorted them through the night.

At the end of the day, when the litter bins around Westminster burst with abandoned placards, only a few of them are left as they head to the brewery underneath the National Theatre, not far away from their old student dorms. Giulia dated Elliott for a few months but today he is holding Hana's hand. Nick is here as well, his hair getting longer every year. Candice has a baby wrapped against her belly. Jane and Nathan are holding hands as newlyweds do. They walked all day, chanting, dancing, dispersing into small groups to catch up on lost time. They wrapped up some more so they could stay outside, standing around one of the concrete tables, lighting cigarettes, a continuous stream of chatter and beer between them. Each one of the stories they share triggers a summarising introduction, a justification almost, for the friends who know more about the younger versions of themselves than they do of their present selves. They sigh and they promise not to leave as much time in between their next encounters, even though they inevitably will, commutes and work and lack of sleep getting in the way. Enclosed between the imposing concrete building and the water from the river, on this crisp shared day with past friends, they are embraced by the comfort of paused time; the alcohol slowly makes their brains lighter, their hearing decreases as they step away from the songs of the march, their sharp sight blurs. They try to remember the name of the quiet girl on their floor in their student halls; they howl with laughter at the memory of Jane being thrown out of a club in Soho after she tried to haggle her round of shots; they stay quiet for a few minutes after remembering James, their friend who crashed his car into a wall; there are more tears when Nick confesses he was madly in love with Nathan, of laughter this time; they cannot quite believe how similar Candice and her baby look; there is a sudden, thicker texture to the air when Hana reveals she thought Sophie and Claude were in a relationship when they first met. Nobody knows how long Claude and Sophie have known each other. Candice is the one who breaks the ice and asks Sophie how Dean is and why has he not joined them today. She assures her that it would have been nice to see him as well, her lips curving after her words fall silent, a whispering *for once* hangs in the air. Sophie's drinking pace quickens, and soon after Claude escorts her to a cab. A paused second – Sophie's eyes meet Claude – she steps inside the car. When diligent Claude returns, a small group decides to walk along the water towards London Bridge for more drinks. And dinner, insists Giulia. She is filing for her residency but swears she is moving back to Italy every single time they are out and refuse to have food.

'You guys have a serious issue with liquid meals,' she roars as she reads through the menu. Nathan walks her to the bar next, to order another round of drinks and some food to share, 'other than crisps,' Giulia mutters.

'So what's up with Soph?' Nick asks Claude directly.

'She is quite overworked, I think. Nothing new.'

Nick starts scrolling on his phone but Jane is eager to hear more about Sophie. The relationship between the two women grew at an unequal pace, the consequence of both an empathy that comes with shared experiences and envy. Jane exchanges a glance with Claude before she adds, hesitantly: 'She's gotten quieter. You guys OK?'

'Yeah. I mean we're both fine. Separately. It's not uni days anymore, we both have our own lives to get on with.'

'You guys are cute,' adds Nick, before putting his phone down in the middle of the table, the screen facing up. 'What do you think of this guy? A little Waitrose, but cute, right?'

Jane nods, Nick swipes right, Nathan and Giulia return and the friends grow loud around the small table. Claude sits back in her seat, her eyes and fingers focus on the tides curling in her pint of beer.

2013, there was a constant taste of alcohol in our mouths when we moved out of halls. I moved first, to Walthamstow, so Sophie took up her mother's offer soon after. She bought a flat in one of the warm newly built buildings in Mile End, 'a great first step on the property ladder.' Sophie was dating Dean already, had been ever since our first year of university. They were spending an increasing number of hours together – but when I asked if he had moved in, Sophie denied it. I was working longer shifts to afford my rent and Sophie was studying for her final exams, ushering me through the door of flamboyant after-parties across London. We saw less of our past friends. We learnt new names more often. Sophie swept through rooms graciously, wearing little dresses and high heels. I didn't belong there, my lips sticky instead of shining, my curves and flat hair on display, my hands firmly pressing against my hips, tightening myself. I drank more but stuck to liquid. Sophie upgraded to other substances, in the form of pills and powder, juggling her compact mirror and lipstick to sculpt the reminiscences of our past, shared girlhood. We spoke less but every interaction we had felt more intense than it ever had before. I still feel pain in my bones when I think back to Sophie on the bus journeys home, peeling the skin around her almond-shaped fingernails, grinding her teeth. She is so fragile, my Sophie, once the curtains are drawn.

Night has landed over the sticky pub table, launching Giulia and Nathan's ceremonial argument. 'But, Giulia, who is going to pay for all these precious subsidies?'

'The rich.'

'That's ridiculously naive of you.'

'What? To ask for the right to afford a roof over my head, not to worry about falling sick, for everyone to have some spare change to go to university? Does that sound naive to you?'

'It's idealistic. Idealistic is what he meant,' interjects Jane. Nathan nods and throws his back down against the chair, too tall, his legs are enlacing the others', his upper body moving from left to right in an attempt to finally settle. It makes him look nervous, pushing Jane to the edge, satisfying Giulia. Claude has noted their role play, still posing quietly in the background. She shares Giulia's opinion, broadly, she simply cannot be bothered to argue about this, not here, not now. 'À quoi bon,' she mutters, what is the point of arguing in an echo chamber.

Giulia continues, 'We need a limit on how wealthy a person can be. Above that, it goes to charities and other trust funds. Easy.'

'But, Giulia, think a little.' Nathan takes another sip from his drink, hands trembling, a few drops spilling down his cyan-blue shirt. 'You're being counterintuitive. You want to support the right to earn a salary on merit but at the same time, you want to cut out thousands of pounds from other people's earnings.'

'Nathan, I do not think anyone,' she pauses to meet his eyes, 'any *man* is deserving of billions of pounds.'

Nick and Claude burst into laughter.

'Touché,' adds Jane.

Giulia continues, 'All I'm saying is that the system is broken. It relies on what we call unskilled workers to work harder for a more precarious outcome. The result is simple: the workforce is exhausted, and the economy is even more unbalanced.'

'We get it, the class system is a bitch. Put the queer people in power. Claude, what do you think?'

Claude stays still. Everyone else rolls their eyes, granting Nathan a rest before he continues: 'Great contribution, Nick, thanks.' His tired eyes return to Giulia. 'You have a point about the exhausted workforce. But the solution is in labour regulations, not in taking away income from a part of the population.'

Giulia leans towards Nathan, her eyes sparking. 'You can't shit money, right? You said it yourself earlier. Where do you get it if not out of the pockets that are already full?'

'I can't argue with you communists. Anger always wins over pragmatism.'

'Yeah, Nath, being dirt poor when I work full-time makes me angry.'

The table plunges into silence and Claude makes her way to the bar.

We met Giulia a year or so later, at the house party that turned our lifelong duo with Sophie into a threesome. When we pushed through the front door, Sophie had promised me another memorable Saturday night: we found an overcrowded flat and a woman standing in the middle of the room. Everything else was spinning on the back of the techno music beat, forced smiles on the guests' faces as they craved a good time. Giulia was wearing a sequin dress, with big black boots, a high bun loosely holding her curly hair and a popping red lipstick. She was rolling a cigarette. The colour on her nails was worn-out. Nothing seemed to matter to her. Can she even hear the music? I thought. Sophie introduced us.

'Lady Danger?' Small pause. Sophie repeated herself: 'Your lipstick, I recognise it, it's called Lady Danger.'

She smiled, her eyes focused on her rolling fingers, 'You're a connoisseur.'

'I'm a make-up artist. Sophie. And this is Claude.'

'Giulia. Do you guys know Tom?'

'Who's Tom?' Sophie replied.

'I don't know. I figured someone must be called Tom. I just moved into the flat next door, heard the music and thought I should come in. You know, to meet people.'

Sophie side-eyed me with a smile I knew too well at the time, the one when she met a daring woman who promised her good memories. Neither of us bothered to tell Giulia the party was for our friend Nick's birthday. Sophie picked up the conversation: 'Where are you from?'

'Bologna.'

'Claude, why don't you make Giulia a gin and tonic?'

I offered her wine as an alternative. The bottles and cans made coarse, jostling noises as I bent downwards to reach for my bag.

She nodded at the wine bottle before adding: '"Claude". That's not very British.'

'*Do you know Claude Cahun?*' *interrupted Sophie.*

Motionless, Giulia looked at me, '*Are you a photographer, then?*'

And so I introduced myself: '*Not so much. My mother is French, though, hence the name. I work in a restaurant.*'

'*A French cook,*' *Giulia announced, rolling her* '*r*' *more than she had done so far, a sign of camaraderie.* '*I work in hospitality too.*'

'*Waitressing,*' *we bonded.*

'*For now.*' *Sophie raised her glass.* '*Claude's a great cook. It's only a matter of time.*'

'*So, you'd like to be a chef?*'

I shrugged and looked back to Sophie. '*A baker, I guess. I like to bake and to ferment stuff.*'

Claude returns with small tumblers, salt and lime: 'To being adults!'

'And dirt poor!' adds Nick.

As she raises her shot of Tequila, Giulia remembers her mother's proud eyes when she left Italy for London, the first woman in her family to attend university. Claude nods back, twinkling at her.

2

'Don't buy this shithole.'

Giulia taps her shoulder against Sophie's. 'Souvenirs, souvenirs,' she hums. 'She is a sentimentalist. Let her be. And don't we all love to hang out in here?'

Giulia meant her question to be rhetorical but Sophie interrupts, 'Love is not a reason to go bankrupt.'

'Fair. But do you girls remember the day we decided to paint the bathroom in that awful apple green? Or the hours we spent trying to close the window in the living room fully so we wouldn't freeze to death in winter? I love it here.'

Claude smiles silently.

The dinner party they have the evening after Claude sends off the final mortgage paperwork is one to remember. At the table, within the safety of walls Claude now owns, fears evaporate. The flat looks nothing like the dream house Claude and Sophie had made mind maps of together when they were children, but Sophie is clearly relieved her friend is settling down. Giulia, in return, is not so angry at homeowners anymore. Claude was right, she tells her, to invest the money she inherited from her grandmother. A chill runs down their spines when someone mentions Mamie, the woman who donated her house in her will, a woman none of them has ever met in person, not even Claude. The will without which buying a house in London would have never been possible.

Claude had considered moving to France a few times, the country she knows mainly through postcards and her mother's unreliable memory. She itched with a sense of duty to keep the *family house*, to light the gas in her grandmother's kitchen even though she had never called her Mamie directly. They did not know each other much, apart from the packages she sent her granddaughter on notable occasions, and through the paperwork for Claude's mother, paying the rent for her institutionalised bed. But that is strong enough to band together two women, and isn't family about the thread of memories knitted together in living? A family is built by carrying on together – one begins by making the first stitch for the other members to add their stitches to, emerging from the same roots. Slipping loops, needles moving, yarn weaving over and under, as the family paces through life events, transferring the loop on to the other threading needle. It is what matters then: to create future memories despite the fear of generating knots, of losing continuity; to become a family as new stitches appear. It is tiring to remember, so very tiring. Claude can still hear the fast-paced little sobs her mother was making the morning they came to pick her up for the first time.

On the day they are due to warm the house Claude has been living in but now officially owns, Sophie and Giulia drive to Whitstable first thing in the morning. They have sourced a vintage oyster plate from an online marketplace as a housewarming present. A brilliant idea, except without oysters to serve, the plate would have looked lonely. It is big enough to accommodate twelve oysters – a dinner for one, or four oysters each as an appetiser. A glorious green, straight from Provence, it also has a lumpy texture so the oysters don't slide away, or so the description reads. The wider outer circle can accommodate ten oysters. The smaller inner circle is made for the two remaining oysters and for two half lemons. It screams Claude to them.

Sophie jumps in the car, wrapped up in an oversized beige woollen scarf. 'It's not the most sustainable thing we've ever done. Claude is going to lecture us for sure.'

'What's worse: to buy unethical oysters from the supermarket or to drive back and forth to the seaside to pick up responsibly farmed ones?'

They are silent at first, feeling faint at the size of the problem they have created for themselves, until they break into laughter. The small orange car jiggles and Giulia resumes, 'Seriously, I do wonder.'

'Where would the supermarket's oysters come from? We could start with comparing distances.'

'But we need to consider that one cargo is for hundreds of oysters together. We are only driving twelve native oysters back. I mean, I have space in the boot for more but have you got Dean's credit card?' Giulia waits for a signal; Sophie rolls her eyes. They both snort.

'Seriously,' interrupts Sophie as she takes her phone out of her jeans pocket. She begins mumbling as she types, 'Oysters. We would have gone to . . . Waitrose, right? Well, they would have been more sustainable for our wallet, that's for sure. They sell *Crassostrea gigas*, also called Pacific oysters. Do you know your oysters, Juddy?'

Only Sophie calls Giulia *Juddy*. The nickname takes them back to one of their early drunken nights, when Lady Gaga sang 'Bad Romance', Rihanna called out her 'Rude Boy' and Ke$ha reminded them it was time to go home with 'TiK ToK'. They were both walking up Hackney Road, falafel wraps dripping in their hands: 'Giulia? You're my buddy for life. Mmmh. Wait, you are my *Juddy.*' Since then they have forgotten many nights out, along with the disappointments and other life upsets that brought them to the dance floor in the first instance, but Juddy makes for five memorable letters that resisted the exercise of time passing.

'I know nothing about oysters, babe. Claude always speaks about this book she adores, what is it? With the silvery shiny oyster on the front page?'

'*Consider the Oyster.* M. F. K. Fisher. Her idol.'

'I wish Claude were here. She'd know.'

'We're surprising her. Okay, so I found the Shellfish Association of Great Britain's report about the Pacific oyster in the UK. *Economic, Legal, and Environmental Issues Associated with its Cultivation, Wild Establishment and Exploitation.* Sounds legit.'

Sophie continues to scroll down her screen while Giulia

quietly focuses on the road. 'Crap, it's from 2012,' mutters Sophie, before returning to the article.

Giulia loves to drive with Soph since her radio doesn't work; she has this capacity to focus her mind on one subject only, digging further, asking more questions, which accompanies them through all of their journeys. She chit-chats as she goes. Giulia doesn't have much to do: she only drives, in silence, thinking about her mother who once drove all the way from Croatia to Bologna, pregnant, almost thirty years ago. Giulia, the dutiful daughter, may have flown into London but she had to save money to buy a car soon after she moved. It made her feel safe the same way the fire blankets that hang on the walls in old theatres do. With Claude, it is a different kind of drive: they stay silent for most of it. Both drifting away in their minds, staring out through the windscreen. However wordless they might be together, there is a sense of closeness building up between these two. Their friendship is rooted in what is not said nor explained. Giulia knows the weight of that very silence is something Sophie is frightened by – the lack of control over what is being thought of her. She must analyse and label before others do, and so she let Sophie defend her choice of twelve native oysters as a gift for Claude today.

'The last thing I need to figure out,' Sophie says to Giulia with satisfaction in her voice, 'is if the native oysters of Whitstable are sold near us in London. If not, we can reassure Clo this is the most ethical and delicious gift we could find. The *Crassostrea gigas* oysters are non-native species, considered invasive, and mass-produced: around twelve hundred tonnes are produced each year in the UK, of which sixty-seven per cent is exported across the globe. From France to Southeast Asia.'

'Wait. If they are from Japan originally, why are they produced in the UK to be sent back to Southeast Asia?'

Sophie grins triumphantly. 'Because they are worth more than ten million pounds to the British economy.'

'Madonna!'

'Consider the oyster, rightly so, Fisher!' They both laugh until they tear up and fall back into a short silence, a roadmap of opportunities and dead ends lying before them, nauseous expectations.

'What are we going to do about the champagne?' asks Giulia.

'Screen time is up. We will have to stick to the local booze shop. Surely they sell champagne in Whitstable.'

Giulia briefly thinks about arguing against this screen time limit Sophie sets for herself but never respects. Surely she could break her rule once again and find a nice liquor store for their friend? But they still have half an hour on the road ahead of them: it's not worth the fight. 'Deal. We're almost there.'

When they arrive, they are surprised by how many other people have also driven to the sea this morning. They struggle to find a parking spot. Sophie is growing frustrated at Giulia, who is categorically refusing to pay for parking. It quickly escalates into an argument of principles about wealth and the value of money, culminating with Sophie paying for parking for the day, her credit card nonchalantly meeting the reader as her eyes look forward, and Giulia refusing to buy a coffee, even though she is craving one. They know their friendship always survives this constant defiance, the shared stubbornness that makes them two opposite forces that attract the other. Giulia mostly shares her opinions as they stream through her mind, however undiplomatic or unrealistic they are. Honesty is her proof of respect for otherness. Sophie values Giulia for being outspoken; what she struggles with is when these outbursts take the attention away from her – or when they are not in line with her opinion. But it is a lovely day after all, by the sea and the salt in the air reminds them both of Claude: this quiet, constant existence between them. They miss her when she is not with them. She bears the empathy between the three of them, forever intuitive about what they might need before they do. Claude and the finely chopped anchovy filets she uses to perk up her pasta sauce and spreads. It remains unspoken because they would not dare say this out loud, but Claude is the one looking after them, this much they know. The tension is palpable between the two friends today – the pressure to do the right thing *for Clo*.

Giulia and Sophie drove all the way to the beach early in the morning – isn't that proof of how much they love Claude?

3

Claude bought tulips for the kitchen table. She feels ashamed for not looking at other properties, investigating and researching the market she feels estranged from. She wanted to give her pennies and feel safe in exchange, that's all. The small flat on Fleeming Road has been the 'headquarters' of their friendship, as declared by Giulia one drunken night on the unsafe but conquered rooftop. They don't lock the door when they go to the bathroom; they all fill up the fridge as if it is theirs, pinning receipts to the door and never doing the maths; they borrow books from the 'library' as they wish, returning them annotated even though they never discuss any of them out loud. Claude hangs posters from every single exhibition she attends, asymmetrically and frameless, through-out the place. It is crowded but that is how she creates a sense of shelter: the corridors, the bathroom, the living room, all showcasing time passing, souvenirs of a life in the making. She loves her flat. She recycles the fish tins her grandmother sends her from Brittany, soap plates, junk jars, ashtrays. She owns this horrific rug a friend once gave her. Nobody knows why she has kept it all these years but there is no talking Claude out of it. She can hear Sophie, a cigarette in hand, *Clo, this rug is terrible for my asthma. The dust, Claude, it's unbearable.* She pictures Giulia, clicking her fingers, sly eyes.

Should we set fire to it? It's kind of chilly in here. Sophie and Giulia bursting into laughter and Claude heading back to the kitchen to grab another bottle of wine. In the yellow kitchen, Claude ferments asparagus, onions and radishes through the seasons and market's offers. Sophie finds it creepy and Giulia hasn't noticed. What they both know about Claude's cooking is the taste of the pistachio and aniseed cake, the sardine and chilli spaghetti, the spinach quiche. On the shelves sit jars, where Claude meticulously tidies and dates her stocks of basmati, brown and jasmine rice; plain, corn, wholemeal and almond flours; chickpeas, green and butter beans, coarse and icing sugars. She keeps and sterilises empty jam jars to store spices – cumin, turmeric, paprika, za'atar – and also cashews, pecans, walnuts. On the window sill grows basil, thyme and oregano. What you will never find in Claude's kitchen is coriander, because Sophie thinks it tastes like soap.

Earlier this morning, Claude cycled to the shops on a quest for cornstarch and cream of tartar to make a lemon meringue tart. The lemons were bruised. She found a crate of straw-berries, however, flamboyant and succulent-looking. She walked back home, next to her bike, her strawberries under her right arm. She can't wait to send a picture to Sophie; she loves their sweetness. Claude cannot quite shake the anxiety of tonight's dinner, the pressure for it to be special and familiar at the same time. She settles her stomach with some oatcakes and Comté cheese before she starts working her dough. She grabs a bowl from one of the open shelves to combine the flour and icing sugar. Slowly, with bare hands, she incorporates the butter. This is exactly when she realises that buying this small and failing flat was the right choice. She does not really care about how messy her baking is becoming, sticky butter between her fingers, flour snowing around. She continues to work the dough as the excitement for Giulia and Sophie to arrive grows: soon they will be home too. The dough is now shaped into a thick disc and packed in cling film, chilling in the fridge, a little sunshine from the beaten egg and butter coming together. Meanwhile she carries on, cutting strawberries, creaming butter with granulated sugar, mixing the eggs and adding ground almonds. She tastes as she goes, playing with the overall texture of the filling. She is looking for a balance – Sophie loves it sweet, Giulia likes it a little undercooked and Claude loves the frangipane the most. She dusts the dark oak kitchen table with flour, ready to roll out her pastry, when she is inter-rupted by the doorbell.

Claude runs downstairs. 'J'arrive!'

'Ciao!' Giulia and Sophie yell in unison behind the door. All the concerns they had shared about Claude buying the place – the damp in the bathroom, the single-glazed windows, the papier-mâché-like walls, the wobbly shelves – are gone. It is what she needs, a nest, four walls to hold on to the idea that they will be friends for ever. Claude opens the door and finds them holding a huge box, a greasy blue bag with a fishy smell permeating from it, one bottle of champagne and two bottles of Sauvignon Blanc. Giulia is wearing black leggings; Sophie is wearing simple high-rise blue jeans, showing her ankles and glittery socks. Claude has put on her favourite loose black trousers, with a vintage yellow shirt tucked in.

'What's that smell?'

Giulia leads the way inside as Sophie begins to reveal: 'We took a small detour today.'

'Via Whitstable!'

Claude rolls her eyes, towards Sophie first and then Giulia, intrigued, curious to know more.

Sophie continues, 'You'll understand when you open your gift. We didn't really know how to wrap it, so pardon the cardboard box.'

'I mean what would a housewarming party be without some cardboard boxes floating around?' Giulia's dry humour is difficult to appreciate if one cannot see her daring look as she speaks.

They arrive on the second floor, out of breath from the fast-paced talking. Claude opens the box and screams for joy. Sophie begins to slide open the drawers, in search of a bottle opener. Giulia runs to the small laundry room and comes back with a hammer.

'It's time we space out those shelves. It's your place now, you're entitled to an upgrade to wine glasses and oyster plates.'

While Claude puts the tart in the oven, Giulia begins to rearrange the shelves and Sophie sips her wine, giving directions about which shelves should go and the ones that need to stay. As soon as Claude sits at the table, reunited with her mug of wine, Sophie starts telling her about the men who served them the oysters that morning: the hard skin along the defined lines of their hands; how fast they opened shells for the long queues of Londoners who had come to enjoy the salty air. They told them they would do this job for as long as they could hold a knife: it has been running in the family for as long as there have been photographs to make a record.

Claude interrupts, 'That makes me feel better. To know that you gave some business to deserving people, because it was not the most sustainable thing you could do,' she drinks more wine before continuing, 'to drive all the way to Whitstable for twelve oysters.'

Giulia and Sophie burst into uncontrollable and loud laughter, and for a split second, Claude is unsure if she is in her kitchen, or theirs. Sophie notices her worried look, 'Sorry, Clo. We just knew you would say that.'

'This exact sentence,' Giulia corrects her.

Sophie reports on their research, about the *Crassostrea gigas* from the London supermarkets, about how far they travel, back and forth, about the overall stain they have on the economy and on the maritime flora. Giulia insists again that it was the most ethical thing to do, if not sustainable per se.

'Do you not like our gift, then?' asks Sophie.

Claude is looking at her from the other side of the table – Sophie has already drunk two glasses of wine when Giulia and she are only halfway through their first. Her friend's cheeks are bony, her teeth make rare appearances, her hair looks thinner than ever. She wishes it was the two of them, only for a few minutes, so she could squeeze her hands and ask her what is really going on. Only the two of them, so she could hear the truth. The pair of them, so Sophie would eat something.

Giulia is still hammering in the background, telling them about this guy she has been texting on the latest dating app she has subscribed to. This app feels more human, she tells them. You have to fill out a questionnaire when you first register, with questions that force you to consider others in the process too. Why do you want a partner? Why now? What kind of compromises are you ready to make? The guy is called Teddy.

'That's a good enough reason to say no,' says Sophie.

Claude clicks her tongue against the roof of her mouth. Giulia continues: he is Australian and moved to London about ten months ago, he works in advertising and plays basketball. He is suggesting they meet for a beer on Tuesday evening, somewhere around King's Cross as they both work in the area. Sophie determines this date a waste of time; Claude argues she has nothing to lose. They are looking at each other, Giulia working away on the shelves.

'All done,' she says as she wipes her forehead. 'Hey, love-birds, look at the shelves! I can't believe it took us years to finally get around to doing this.'

'Thank you, Giulia. I will have to buy wine glasses now.'

'Let me steal some from Allegra's kitchen next time I go up to Hampstead. I think we're going for lunch next Sunday with Dean.'

Half of the furniture and various objects Claude owns already come from Sophie's mother's house. Sophie simply grabs them and brings them back to her friend's flat, slowly building a safer space for those recollections of her childhood. The selection of objects varies from books, picture frames, small odd sculptures from gift shops around the country to practical tools such as a bread knife, bottle rack and even the hammer Giulia used to fix the cupboards. Allegra spends so little time in the house herself, her days and nights shared between work and after-work parties, that she never seems to notice. She never mentions the missing bits if she does.

They eat the oysters, small sounds of disgust slipping out as they do. Sophie posts the most perfect photo of the oyster plate and champagne bottle on her Instagram profile. Dean texts soon after to ask if she is staying at Claude's overnight. She quickly replies that she is. They pop the champagne for the thrill of it, but they don't drink much. They don't like bubbles and it gives Claude headaches. Soon after, Giulia is turning the music up from her phone, the radio has fallen silent again tonight; Sophie talks about her work, angry as usual at her boss and his patronising emails at all hours of the day, while Claude sweats over the hob. She is cooking crab pasta — it is tomatoey for Giulia and not too spicy for

Sophie. Soothed by the chatter from her friends in the background, Claude is stirring the sauce, drifting away.

The years when we had to take off our shoes before entering the dormitory, when no food was to be taken outside the canteen, when lights had to be switched off thirty minutes after we went upstairs. In 2006, at the Rosary Boarding School on the edge of the Kent Downs, with its bunk beds staged at the end of a long and creaking corridor, I met Sophie. We wore uniforms back then, pink bubblegum tangled in our braces, braided hair running down our backs. Sophie dropped like a parcel midway through Year 9, constant goosebumps highlighted her peach fuzz, the name of her parents introduced her in glory before she even made an entrance. Allegra and Mark Cruwys, the fashionable letters, the taste that runs magazines; the parents who travelled too often to raise their own child. I remember the notice that instructed us to get dressed and undressed within the shelter of the one screen in the dorm, leading us to queue docilely first thing in the morning and last thing in the evening, the radiators attached to the walls switched off, our raw hands rubbing our eyes. Then there were the nights of extreme cold in winter or amidst the hot summers when Sophie's night terrors came back to her; the nights when Sophie delicately levelled her body next to mine, under the thin blanket. We started to build a dream of a shared house in Provence, where the warming sun would bring us together and the fields of lavender would protect us from our fears. We had to stay close so the other girls would not catch us when our bodies aligned against one another, our bones stiff from the fear of waking the mattress springs. The night when Sophie quietly landed her lips on mine.

'Now who wants whisky with their dessert? I made a strawberry and almond tart.'

Claude launches herself towards the bottle before they have time to answer the obvious. They have dessert and then more whisky. Their conversation hovers between the micro and the macro events of their lives: Giulia's stepbrother is graduating at the end of this term; is this new raspberry lipstick appropriate for the office; how is Sophie's business plan shaping up; Meghan and Harry had a baby; how is Dean, Brexit, Extinction Rebellion? Giulia on the sofa and Sophie in the bed, they soon fall asleep while Claude washes up the dishes, making as little noise as possible.

She misses the extra shelving space.

Claude has been feeling uneasy all day. Mondays at the coffee shop end with tired eyes and restless hands – not as many mouths to feed but double-zero entries to fill on the stocklists. To record stock into a log is not a problem, this suits her organised mind, it is the anxiety that comes with the listing she dreads. The possible opportunities in sight: the meals that are waiting to be cooked from these ingredients. Is it wise to use this much flour for the blueberry buns this week? Should they set more aside for the focaccia? What if the mood is more on the bitter side? Should they move things around in the fridges for this week's worth of food to fit? She does the stocklist in the backroom, sitting on the hard floor between the boxes of wine, even throughout winter. It keeps her mind focused and alert. None of her colleagues can read her handwriting apart from Sasha, who she employed almost two years ago. Sasha knocked on the door one afternoon, following up on the small notice that was taped to the vitrine – *looking for a busser, part-time, come in for more details*. Claude asked what she would do with two eggs and anything else she wants. Sasha didn't think twice before she replied, *an omelette*. They smiled at the prospect of simplicity in their lives, at the beauty of having two eggs to beat, as easy as that. Claude recognised the relentless pragmatism in which the life of a single mother is enclosed. Sasha started the following Monday. The small business is doing well and Claude has all the freedom she could wish for since the owner moved to Spain for his retirement, only visiting once a year. It gives her enough time to do her own deliveries on the side. She does not turn off the lights at the end of the day; instead she stays in the kitchen and begins her second shift, baking her bread and other pastries, sourcing butter all the way from Brittany. This is what she had come to London for in the first place, why she dropped out a few weeks into her third year. Claude wanted to use her hands to create something tangible so she quit university and took on a job at the café. They already had a chalkboard to feature their daily changing menu then, and she grew to enjoy the sound of chalk drawing letters on a board as soon as she started conquering the kitchen during the nights. She had wanted to become a baker since she made her first cake, her nostrils over-whelmed, hands rolling fast, launching a future of working dough, pairing otherwise foreign traditions, making some-thing good for others. Claude never leaves the kitchen when one of her creations is rising in the oven. She sits tight in front of the humming machine, flicking through food maga-zines, staring at her dream of a life, a moist dough baking, a truce between the world and herself. Nobody knows about the coffee shop's nightlife apart from Sasha, who loves the free goods from Claude. She has been a single mother to Samsara since the age of seventeen and brings her daughter to the café often. Samsara is at ease in the kitchen, running around, avoiding the knives as she has been advised, scooping leftovers from the overnight mixing bowls. Claude has agreements with a few families around North London, from Sophie, and mainly from Allegra's network, her cakes popping up on dressed tables at adults' and children's birthday parties alike. After her shifts on Tuesdays and Thursdays, and the extra clandestine hours in the kitchen, she jumps on her bike, ties on a small trailer, and leaves loaves of bread and tarts of seasonal fruits at their front doors. She is off on Wednesdays and Sundays, when Sasha and Samsara run the café on their own.

As she leaves the backroom, ready to log the stocks on the computer and ask Sean the barista to write this week's menus on the blackboard, in elegant cursive, her phone picks up the 4G again:

GUARDIAN LIVE – BREAKING NEWS – NOTRE DAME DE PARIS IS ON FIRE

With a pounding heart, she swipes for more information. She is late catching up, and finds relief in learning the organ is reported to have been spared. She shakes her head: *how tragic*, she thinks. She doesn't play the organ, she doesn't even know what it sounds like, and yet she is so affected by the prospect of the city's singing heart being turned into ashes. Will there be an organ at the ceremony when Sophie marries

Dean? She bets Allegra will secure them a renowned organist. She must know one.

It was only this past Saturday, on a warm April evening, that Sophie picked Claude up at the café. She was holding two cans of gin and tonic in her hands, her long body lying against the counter. They walked home together that night, Claude's bike between them, the pedals scratching their ankles every other step. It wasn't so much of a surprise to find Sophie outside the café after her shift. This was a recurring habit they had, walking together to the pub around the corner for a wine-infused catch-up. The bartender has learnt to hand over a mixed bowl of green and black olives with their bottle of Côtes du Rhône. But that Saturday felt different, when she found Sophie biting her nails. It was not the bitten nails that caused Claude dismay. Sophie has always done this and Claude is still repelled by the feeling of Sophie's little nails scratching her bare legs as she slid under the duvet back in school. She has never told Sophie this, it would break her heart to learn that she leaves worrisome tracks behind. It took Claude another few seconds until she noticed the big, green, three-dimensional jewellery circling her left fourth finger. Sophie was hopping up and down by then, a wide smile across her face.

'It's a diamond!' she screamed.

'Oh, Sophie!' Claude gasped for air as she came closer to hug her oldest and best friend. 'I want to hear everything.'

And Sophie interrupted her: 'Yes, he went down on one

knee.' She continued to jump around, making Claude dizzy until she caught her hand, 'good boy.'

Sophie settled back on her feet and pushed her ornamented finger through Claude's hand and their fingers intertwined. 'Allegra said Holly Golightly would have disapproved, because *it's tacky to wear diamonds before you're forty; and even that's risky.* But she is proud of me. She's calling people today. It's going to be grand.'

Claude squeezed her friend's hand. 'Should we walk back to mine? I have everything we need to make a celebratory pasta.'

The next day Sophie left early, returning to Dean who was growing more impatient by the hour. Claude began to clean the flat. First, she put the bed sheets into the wash – cotton cycle, 60°C – then she went around the house and opened every single window, wind entered and doors slammed behind. She wanted as much air as possible; she did not care about the doorframes. Gloveless, her skin cracking from the bleach, she began with the bathroom, guided by an unconscious routine. She made sure to scrub everything, even the grout: she cannot stand its orange tone. She continued on to the toilet, and next she hung the laundry to dry in the bay window, where the sun always is the warmest. She dusted the shelves and surfaces in her bedroom and living room. She started vacuuming and mopping the floors. Then she put the Moka pot on. The kitchen was still dirty from the night before, the pots and oven trays soaking in vinegar, and the once hot water had turned cold. Morning had broken with the need to open a new jar of jam; Claude sat at her table, fresh butter uncovered. *I was four, perhaps five, sitting on the high stool by the kitchen counter. Maman was moving in circles around the room, waiting for the toast to turn gold, anxious at the wait and growing smell of burn. She grabbed the jam jar; it was fresh from the shop. She knelt on the floor and tapped the lid against the tiles until it made a sharp, unexpected noise — pop! — and I exploded into baby-like laughter. I contaminated Maman, who too laughed, an exquisite nursery rhyme.*

Claude cherishes that moment — this one practical tool she has learnt from her mother, how to unseal a jam jar. She loves that the unsealing is an abrupt movement, one which fits alongside the other memories she holds of her mother. These come to Claude while she washes the dishes, while she walks, while she picks up something that fell on the floor, while she brushes her teeth — the recollection always taking the form of a sudden flashback, a hasty slap of memory.

The morning after Sophie shared the news of her engagement with Dean, she ate her toast with the noise of the crumbs falling back on the plate for sole company. Claude went to clean the kitchen next: she was leaning over the hob when the doorbell rang. She wasn't expecting anything but her bet was on Giulia, who often directs her parcels to Claude's as she doesn't trust her flatmates. She didn't bother to put herself together for the delivery person. When Claude opened the door, it was Allegra she found – blunt-cut bob, Jacquard-weave suit, an oversized shopping bag before her feet. They stayed silent for as long as it took them to acknowledge the time that had passed in between their encounters, scars on their skin, wrinkled hands, the marks of the passing years, more obvious in Claude's case. The gospel of their relationship had always been bouncing back between life events and Sophie's choices, Allegra the pillar for a rotating orbit, the woman before the girls.

'Hi Allegra, what a surprise,' said Claude as she bent down to grab the bag, following Allegra's pinched smile and authoritative eyes, which had gravitated towards Claude's fading welcoming doormat. They both entered the flat and Claude apologised for the state of the kitchen, suggesting they settle on the sofa instead. As they stepped into the room, she remembered the linen sheets she had put away to dry earlier. The room had shrunk, the air had become harder to breathe; she was sweating and aware of it. Allegra said not to worry but did not widen her smile. She suggested Claude open the box now.

'Sophie often tells me about the nights she spends watching you bake at the café. I thought you could do this best alone in the comfort of your own home. My friends enjoy your tarts. Mia sang the praises of the apricot one the other day. Her kids adored it. Congratulations on buying the flat, by the way.' Claude was softly running her kneading fingers across the turquoise stand mixer, unsure of the value of such a gift.

'Thank you. You just missed Sophie.' Claude looked at this woman she knew so little about, but who had shadowed her growing up, a figure of both respect and fear. She did not lower her gaze when Allegra began her monologue. She had spoken to *charming* Dean about the wedding this morning. They were so excited about the day – *Have you saved the date already, Claude?* They would love for her to bake the wedding cake; they will pay for her labour, of course they will. It needs to be special so it would be *terrific* if she could gather some thoughts and send an email to both Dean and herself. *Would a thousand pounds be enough, not counting the cost attached to the ingredients?* They will cover that separately as she wants to make sure it's all sourced from the best British producers. *The butter must come from Sussex.* She has no notion of a fair price so she would be grateful if Claude could have a think. They are so very excited – what a delightful prospect to have her daughter Sophie married to the wonderful Dean. *I suppose you have seen the diamond, Claude? It hasn't been the easiest of years for Sophie, so it is important we all do what's best for her.* Claude was nodding, half listening, half wondering if Soph made it safely back to Mile End. Would they be moving into a bigger house? Claude wondered. Sophie hated that flat.

'Do you have a venue in mind already?'

'Does that influence the process of making the cake?' The question almost sounded genuine. Allegra could make you doubt anything, even your own ability to decide if you are thirsty or not. Claude's throat started to itch.

'Not as such. I was just curious.'

'Sophie will be thrilled that you are making her wedding cake. We will keep this a surprise for now, shall we?'

Claude nodded. They stayed silent for a minute before Claude escorted Allegra back to the front door. She did not offer her a cup of coffee. 'What a shame you arrived when I was cleaning the hob and I can't offer you a hot drink.'

'I arrived unannounced, darling. Good day now.' Claude closed the door after Allegra, and slowly slid against it. She had never baked a wedding cake. *They're supposed to have many layers, aren't they?* The prospect of icing sugar turned Claude's stomach upside down.

She composed herself, returned to the hob, and she scrubbed.

5

May arrives and disappears quickly. Claude has not emailed Allegra and Dean about the wedding cake, even though she could use the extra cash; Giulia has passed the tenth date milestone with Teddy and still has a spark in her eye when she mentions his name, a distraction she welcomes as a break from filling spreadsheets and fulfilling none of her dreams at the office; Sophie is looking to buy a house with Dean near Tufnell Park. They all meet in a pub around the area early in the evening on a Friday. Sophie is defeated by the state of the apartments she has visited most of the afternoon, Claude is able to finish early as she was training a fantastic new barista. Giulia arrives soon after, her make-up from the day before hazy, her hair tucked into a bun.

'When are you going to leave some basic products at Ted's?' asks Sophie as soon as Giulia sets three pints in front of them. She is playing with the small splinters from the picnic table.

'Ted's?'

Sophie gives nicknames to everyone. Giulia does not understand her purpose in doing so, and Claude ignores them. 'Teddy, if you prefer.'

'It's his name, not my preference, Soph.' Giulia blushes. 'We're not there yet. I'm happy with things as they are.'

Sophie continues to sound Giulia out about her potential future with Teddy – have they had *the* chat? About exclusivity. Does he check in with her first thing in the morning? Will they go on a short holiday together this summer? Giulia defuses each question, giving Sophie short answers and turning her eyes away from those of her friends, safeguarding the life she leads outside of their trio. Claude looks at the ash tree behind them – imposing, a pop of green. The wind is causing the young leaves to shake, generating a light jingling noise. Back at the Rosary school there was a welcoming oak tree at the bottom of the park, where the girls hid on Saturday afternoons, seeking shelter under the stretching branches. It was spring as well back then, and their bodies were awakening. *I had stopped listening, absently pulling off bits of grass, when Amy suggested we play a new game. Her cousin had warned her: they had to be ready for the summer holidays. The boys would be. The rules are easy, she said, a sticky bottle of milk in her hands, instructing us girls to settle into a small circle. The worried eyes and the bubbling smiles are what I remember most vividly, still today. Amy placed the bottle in the centre of the circle, flattening some of the grass around it. We played rock paper scissors to decide who would initiate. Emma was to spin first and the rest of us focused on the bottle. Amy explained the rules: one person spins the bottle and must kiss the person to whom the bottle points after it stops spinning. The other girls started to giggle but closed their mouths shortly after Amy added the final rule: the girl who is kissed will then grade the kisser, from 0 to 10. They had to be ready for summer camps, she repeated. Every Saturday in the run-up to summertime, we pushed our small lips together, painstakingly finding ways to improve. We trialled coy gestures of warmth with unsteady fingers and soft palms. Small gasps for air, mouths hidden behind our hands, sudden giggles; most of the girls felt like they were breaking the rules.*

Tomorrow is the beginning of a long weekend. The air is warmer, the days are growing longer and brighter. Claude, Giulia and Sophie are women, battling together through life, while their prime minister is announcing her resignation. Theresa May will step down in June. The difficult disappointment in this: how pleasing it should be to be governed by a woman, how shameful to say *good riddance*. They never had the chance to pass on such an opportunity. Sophie is shrinking back, her hand reaching to her stomach. They wish it were different, that politics was not a subject of discord between them, that it would not always swing so personal. Why should they take the blame for a bad government? Why should their friendship suffer from the state of the world? They wish it was summer already, that they had more distractions from the news, cheerful subjects to discuss when they meet. This defeated feeling in their stomachs shortly after they hug goodbye – the drunkest, stinging knowledge that they've spent an entire evening reviewing news in sad tones with tired, downward-looking eyes. They ought to be more fun – better company – to their friends next time. Altogether, these memories they share, and the ones they decide not to share, are the fragments that hold their relationship together, ever threatening to break into a billion tiny pieces. The wary questions they only feel confident to ask after a few drinks. The answers they receive punched with the sweet addition of alcohol, before tomorrow's sour flashbacks. The times they ask how the other feels, sometimes out of consideration but often in hope of being asked the same back. Sophie, Giulia and Claude are three women in the wake of summer 2019: wanting to thrive and often buried under the weight of their own opinions, blinded by the perception they have of themselves, often in disharmony with the one their friends have constructed, putting pieces together, distracted by their own affairs. They are playing the demanding act of aligning their ambitions with what is expected of them. Claude stands up; she is due to get the next round of drinks.

Claude, Giulia and Sophie stay out throughout the night, their minds juggling respective concerns and insecurities, their bodies in togetherness.

Sophie

The first time I went in, it was February. A routine visit but with added dazzle in my stomach; I was there to discuss fertility plans. Dean had kissed me on the forehead as I left the house, 'See you later, Daddy,' I replied. Since then I have been transferred to the university hospital, about forty-five minutes away by train. I go in every six weeks, sit tight in the purple waiting room of the women's clinic, hear my name and then my surname being mispronounced, *Sophie Cruwys*, close my eyes while they do what they have to do, drop off the pink file listing all those molecules I ignore the pronunciation of, yet that make my uterus mine, and head out towards the bookshop around the corner. Painted an eerie azure colour, the shop is a short walk away from the hospital, near enough for my tired legs to reach, far enough not to feel the ambient, contagious worry from the patients anymore.

'Do you often see patients from the hospital?' I ask the

bookseller, a man so tall he seems cramped within the shelves. Slightly awkwardly but tenderly he gets up, and hands me a copy of Elizabeth Strout's *Olive Kitteridge*. 'It will be a comforting read,' he says as he retreats behind the till. I can feel his presence while I run my fingers down the paperback cover. He delicately clears his throat before he continues, 'And if you need more comfort in the future, there is a follow-up coming out later this year, *Olive, Again*.'

I devoured Olive's life, seeking refuge in her community and relief in her anger. I screamed at the stolen shoe. I cried for Olive and Chris to make amends. I went to see the bookseller, whom I soon started to call Alister, every six weeks, reading widely but not grasping most of the words my eyes brushed, my mind constantly distracted. Where do they send those samples – those bits from my uterus? How many people work in those labs? Do they have children of their own? Pets? Do they have hobbies? If only I knew the address of the laboratory. Why can I not read the results for myself? The small numbers and commas lined up on graph paper, the ones that stole ownership from me over the sense of my cells. I hope there is a river near the laboratory. That's a pleasant thought, fluids moving, life flowing.

It began with the word *immature*. My doctor made me lie on the consultation table after I told him Dean and I were ready, that we wanted to start a family together, only my body disagreed. He smiled and said we were going to look into it. The cold gel met my stomach and I could already see us in a few months' time, holding hands as the same textured gel would introduce our child, revealing a newly beating heart between us. I saw the perfect picture; could you have let it go?

The doctor frowned. 'How regular have your cycles been since you stopped the contraceptive pill?'

'I haven't had my period yet. I bled for a few hours, but nothing since. It's been seven months or so, but I was told not to worry too much as it happens when you first quit the pill after a long time on it. It happens to most women.' I was doing my best to encourage him to give me the diagnostic I wanted to be given.

'Your uterus is difficult to reach,' he continued to move the sonogram, 'but the most problematic thing is that it's immature.'

'Immature?'

'It's not completely functioning, hormonally speaking, so your ovulation cycles won't reach their full potential. See here? That's scarring, making your womb and abdominal cavity unwelcoming. I'm afraid it's going to be difficult for you and your partner to conceive naturally. We have treatment plans. I will refer you to the women's clinic for further testing. We want to discount cancer first.'

'Cancer?'

'It could be an unlikely underlying problem.' I heard *unlucky* and he continued: 'Any tiredness?'

Who isn't tired these days, I wondered, before I decided to reply, 'Not particularly.'

55

'Vomiting?'

'No'.

'Unexplained weight loss? Nausea?'

'No.'

'Feeling of vertigo? Imbalance?'

'Emotional or physical?' He finally looked back up, studying my overall appearance, avoiding my eyes. It was so hot; I couldn't think about anything else other than the open window behind his white shirt. The clear, blue sky made London feel higher, the light warming the bay windows of the short Victorian houses.

'Do you sometimes feel faint?'

I wondered how often is sometimes to doctors. 'It happens when I skip breakfast but not for no reason, no.'

'Do you feel unhappy?' What had happened between my train journey, resting my eyes as the sun shone through the window, and that very minute? *Now, I have to know if I'm happy? Do I have cancer? Am I immature, if my uterus is? Do I even want children of my own? Claude says the planet is over-populated already. Is that a fact or an opinion?*

'I have my days, don't we all?' He smiled as he signed the prescription.

'I would also advise couple's therapy. It can be a difficult time, even for the happiest of couples. Trust me.'

He handed me the referral and shook my hand, showing me the way out, my dreams of a life crushed by an ultrasound. I tasted blood in my mouth.

I went straight to Claude's apartment afterwards. On the Tube, I struggled to breathe. I took off my glasses. Put them back on. Rubbed my eyes. Blur. I had never realised we were so many stations apart. Out. Gasped for air. I ran. I couldn't see Claude's apple-green bike outside the house on Fleeming Road. I was frustrated at her absence before I remembered that this is something I adore about her – Claude's weekly routine and how old-fashioned she is. Every Saturday morning, market day, she heads out to her local newsagent, Emin. She convinced him to source *Libération* for her, the single copy was delivered each week on the condition she was going to buy it without fail. She adores the weekend edition. She then goes to her deli, a few meters down the road, for a pastry and a coffee. Now begins my favourite part of this symphony of small leisures or 'petits plaisirs', as she calls them: she does not read any of the articles, instead she meticulously studies the TV schedule. She does not own a television herself, nor does she have a clue what any of these French shows are about.

'It makes me feel cosy to know what families will be doing tonight,' she once explained to me. I had known Claude for years already, we were just out of school. She had introduced herself with a few words about the history of her name. Claude Thomas, gossips and whispers laid out before her, the unwanted child of the history professor, the niece of the director who had a mildly French-sounding name. My heart sank each time she stayed behind, quietly sitting on the floor with a book, while we all queued for one of the two landlines to call home at 6 p.m. Claude only called on Thursdays, when her mother was allowed to answer the phone at her end, from her own room, a whiter, aseptic version of ours. Still, to this day, we do not speak about Claude's mother, only small glimpses of her character seep out through her habits. I have learnt to catch those clues throughout the years, but I still don't understand the thing about the TV schedule.

I looked at the steps in front of her door, where moss was starting to develop with the first autumnal showers. I considered falling flat on them and waiting there for Claude's return, an organic cushion to a clinical day. I decided otherwise and rushed on to the deli. I found Claude by the window. She has this peculiar way of frowning with her eyebrows when she is focusing. She is an individualist, my Clo, and yet she is the most reliable person I know. I pushed the door open. She didn't move despite the sound of the bell announcing me.

'Do you think I'm immature?'

She calmly looked at me, carefully considering her words, assessing my state.

'You opened an ISA with your babysitting money. You've made more business plans than there are entries in the CAC 40. What do you mean by immature? You've always been the one looking ahead for us both, this much I know.' She stood up before I had a chance to answer, her wallet in her left hand. A few minutes later, she was back with our table holder, shaped in the form of a small skittle, the number '4' written in red letters in one hand, a cinnamon bun in the other. 'Here you go. Immature can mean many things, simply undeveloped or showing emotional intelligence that is younger than what is expected for a person of such an age.' She let her words sink in before she continued, 'It's a subjective word, nothing scientific about it. Flat white with oat milk is on the way, that is a fact.'

Claude delicately sliced the bun between us, the crust still soft inside, her forefinger pushing the edge of the plate towards me, her quiet smile and my eyes fixating on her lips.

'What's on the telly tonight?' I asked in return.

'A lot of quiz shows. I struggle to understand why one would want to be reminded of their lack of general knowledge on a Saturday night. A few romantic comedies ahead of Valentine's. Beethoven the St Bernard is still going strong as well.' She paused. 'I do love that dog.' She squeezed my hand tenderly.

'What about reality TV shows, anything good?'

'Oui oui! A bunch of kids are locked in a house together on Channel M6. They all have a secret to keep from the others. I'm not sure how clues are distributed but I expect there is some sort of evil planning involved. The goal is to keep your secret until the very end. Every week the public vote someone out. How tragic would it be to be voted out of your home by millions of strangers?'

'I always think about these kids' mothers.' I paused. 'At least that's one worry I won't have.' The waitress, who was coming through with our coffees, interrupted us. I sipped mine but Claude didn't move. 'Seeing our kids on national TV with Dean, that won't be a thing.'

'I'm sorry, Soph.'

★ ★ ★

I met Dean at a friend's housewarming party, only a few weeks after I moved to London. I was standing still, bored, slowly peeling off the label from my beer bottle, elbows resting against the kitchen counter. I remember that I wore my green silk shirt. I like the movement the texture creates, making me feel rococo, as it slides down against my arms to reveal my bracelets. I never take either of them off and years later, Dean will make sure to match the colour of my engagement ring to them. I only came for Giulia, who had a crush on the host and was in need of a sidekick. I missed Claude. If it were the two of us, we would be screening the room, Claude howling with laughter, she who can be so quiet in intimacy, while I would be contained, aware of my left dimple. Claude is especially good at pairing strangers with an odd hobby, based on the way they move around the room. I love to assign them silly voices and other verbal tics. My head was buzzing already, resting on my hand. We'd started drinking as we picked our outfits and got ready in Giulia's room, one of a five-bedroom house, burgundy stains on our lips. Dean says that I seemed to be daydreaming when he arrived, smiling into the void. I believe him – I still wear this faint, polite smile during social gatherings. *Always act as if someone were going to take an impromptu photo of you*, Allegra used to tell me from her marble kitchen bar in our West Hampstead apartment. Dean was wearing a peacock-blue jumper which highlighted his grey eyes. He moved across the room with a gesture I instantly recognised, one that marked him out as an introvert who steps into a small one-bedroom flat packed with twenty-plus strangers. I knew straight away that he is one to close his bedroom door and not to be seen again until dawn the following day; one to go for long, solo walks; one to stand silently by your side. He embodied safety. He was handsome. I followed him with my eyes as he dropped his pack of beers in the fridge and embraced his friends. I waited, patiently. As soon as he grabbed his coat, I followed him to the balcony. He offered me a cigarette and we smoked, silently. We were in Bethnal Green, facing south. We never went back to that flat and Giulia never saw the guy again, but I remember the Shard distinctively from the skyline.

It was Dean who broke the silence between us first, as he reached out for a second cigarette. 'When I first moved to London, I used to go up the Monument every Tuesday evening after work.' I hadn't expected to hear a Californian accent. 'I can't remember why I started to do it, except that I always hated Tuesdays until I started climbing up there.'

'What made you stop?'

'What makes you think I stopped?'

'You used the past tense.' That was when I finally found the courage to look up, to meet his eyes.

He smiled. 'I moved office.'

'I've never been up the Monument. I was born in London.'

'Do you want to go tomorrow?'

Since then, we've gone up the Monument on the twelfth day of each month. It's a promise we have made to one another. We felt like we were breaking rules, turning into a better version of ourselves as a pair. I sometimes go on my own when I feel trapped in choices I didn't make. I run up the stairs – the 311 steps – and that is when air seems to fill up my cells again, when I reach the top and inhale the view. The first person I think about when I arrive is Claude, quickly followed by my mother, Allegra. I often think about Claude's mother when I go back down the stairs, the same 311 steps in reverse, this woman whose blood pulses through Claude's body. Her hands that have turned purple from washing dishes, calloused from working dough. I never ask Claude about her mother.

To our family and friends, we broke up as summer settled in 2019. It was quick, and Dean moved out of my apartment while I was away in Portugal with Claude and Giulia. It was Claude's birthday weekend, although we were not allowed to call it a birthday celebration. In my heart, we grew apart from the day I came back wounded from the hospital and we became increasingly estranged throughout the process. I woke up in a cold sweat in the middle of the night and all I could picture on the ceiling was the screen on which they displayed my insides at the hospital. Dean slept well throughout, energetically jumping out of bed in the mornings, rushing out to work, to see his mates, to play rugby. *Why is this monitor so big? Isn't it decadent when we know the NHS is running out of cash?* Each time Dean started to trace his fingers down my stomach, I felt the anxiety grow. *I do not want more insertions. No more incisions. I want intimacy.* It all escalated one ordinary and uneventful Sunday. Dean woke up with the look in his eyes and I knew I could not escape any other way than by saying no to him, clearly. I didn't even have the excuse of my periods anymore.

'But how are we going to make a baby if we have sex once every two months?'

He doesn't understand, I realised. In a glimpse of a second, hundreds of small, buried acts rushed back to me: his simple *hmm* after I explained what had happened, the rugby training that fell at the same time as my appointment, the letter marked *private and confidential* he stepped on in the hallway, leaving it behind for me to pick up. A weight made of fear and anticipation lifted from my shoulders. *He doesn't understand and I don't want him to.* Was I supposed to raise those children alone? It was fast. I stood up, jumped into my jeans: 'I'm out. I'm going to Claude's and we're off to Lisbon in two weeks. You have until I get back to move out.' I grabbed my phone as he stayed still. 'That's Monday the 15th.' I sent him an Outlook calendar invitation and then I opened my wardrobe. I packed my bag at such an assured pace that I wondered how long I had unconsciously been preparing for this day. Dean did not say a word. 'I will ask Allegra to call her lawyers. They will take care of the paperwork for the flat so you can get your share back. They'll take care of what needs to be done to break up the engagement.'

I closed the door, entered the lift and stopped the door from closing with my foot. A pause, a breath, before I started my journey downwards. I counted all the way to one hundred; this was how I mourned Dean, dreamlike, the performance of our perfect union. Then I ordered a cab to Claude's house.

Summer

1

Everyone is particular about the order of things along the way to boarding a plane. Giulia needs a special type of hand cream so the 'grossness' from the airport does not stick to her skin, and that specific cream is nowhere to be found despite her thorough search through each one of her bags; Sophie must read the news on paper now and Claude is hunting down a savoury breakfast. Those knife-sharp novelties within each of them are unpleasant. Flying is an individualistic experience, revealing needs that were not so apparent before, out of survival, uncomfortable pointers towards intimate selves, until your elbows align against those of a stranger, until you rely on the person next to you not to fall asleep so you can use the bathroom. To fly with someone you know is to take into account their wary eyes as part of the whole equation.

A few hours deep into a heavy silence between them, Claude, Giulia and Sophie land in Lisbon. The sun burns their skin, Sophie has taken her panama hat out of her smart red suitcase, and Giulia has rolled her sweatpants up to her knees. The mood has lightened, defeated by the warm heaviness in the air. They have travelled to Portugal for Claude's birthday, initially, but now it is more about Sophie and the not-to-be-mentioned broken engagement. Claude repeated the rule to Giulia, who suffocates under the weight of yet another silent agreement between them. They swiftly cancelled the private session they had booked for Sophie to choose her jewellery. Both Claude and Giulia acknowledge that they would have endorsed the union between Sophie and Dean. Another silent agreement, a deal sealed years before. They wanted her to wear something unique and from the pair of them on the day since they could not hold her hands. It would not have appeared proper to Allegra if three women entered the church together, even less so if they walked down the aisle together. Yet it would have felt truthful to Claude – handing Soph over to Dean. She cannot remember the last time she saw Sophie's father, one of the men that fled the present timeline, leaving the women to stitch the fissures back together. Occasionally, Sophie will mention Mark's name, most often as part of her dutiful pact with her mother. *If you are ever asked, Mark is busy building our brand in LA,* is how Allegra had briefed Sophie on the first and last day she dropped her at school. A divorce is not appropriate publicity, even less so for a woman, was the truth. *We are doing this for*

you so you are not judged by the other children, is the excuse
Allegra had given her daughter. The two friends knew that
the day Sophie would have married Dean, she would have
also lost her freedom to run away for a night, to accidentally
fall asleep on Claude's bed after a bottle of wine too many
in the evening. Soon, there would have been nursery songs
calling her home. She would have followed this marriage
through, leaving them no other option than to call it a *success*.
Sophie does what Allegra expects of her, blinkers on, daughter
to her mother. Jewellery seemed more appropriate, and they
had found an artist who sculpts shells into earrings. They
had written a long email about their friendship to the artist,
and she had agreed to book the shop privately for a few
hours for them – for an extra fifty euros, she even ordered
a bottle of champagne. This is now cancelled and they lost
their deposit, and the champagne. They still dislike bubbles.

Giulia has set her mind on using public transport to reach
the holiday home. She runs faster to the vending machines
than the time it takes Sophie to reactivate her 4G and update
her location on her favourite cab app. They will commute
and Claude is smiling: they are on holiday together. On the
train they grow agitated, mistreating their blue travel guide
as they fold down the corners of pages and grab it from one
another's hands. Sophie cannot wait to take pictures on the
Praça do Comércio, Giulia wants to walk along the coast,
all the way to the Belém Tower, Claude is listing the foods
they must taste on her phone's notes app. There is so much

to do. They get off the train, it really is hot, isn't it? They didn't realise Lisbon was so hilly and where is the apartment? They should have arrived by now. Sophie had picked the place, halfway between the beach and the city centre. *Fabulous decor throughout and conveniently located*, the reviews read.

'The kitchen is smaller than it looked in the photos,' Claude declares, her backpack falling down her shoulder. Despite the view overlooking the beach, despite the bathtub, the kitchen is problematic. Sophie glares at Claude, counting in her head, resisting the urge to jump into an argument with her about how irrelevant the kitchen is compared to them being together this weekend. They will eat out anyway, there is a bathtub, the view overlooks the beach, her engagement was broken, why does the kitchen matter so much? Giulia decides to be oblivious and throws her luggage on the sofa with the assurance of one who finds themselves at home. She unzips the bag and digs in, unfolding clothes and random objects, until she finds a packet of breakfast biscuits.

Giulia mutters to herself, 'I don't know why I'm so hungry?'

Claude and Sophie take this as a reference to their argument about breakfast, earlier this morning, at the airport. Giulia categorically refused to eat something savoury, going hungry to prove a point. She tears the packaging apart and picks at the crumbled, smashed oat biscuits. She continues on to the first bedroom and then to the other rooms, slowly experiencing the flat, still snacking, leaving a trail of crunchy little crumbs behind her, until she settles in the bedroom she wants. She walks back to grab her bag, smashing the leftover biscuits into messier stacks. *Tut,* says Sophie in the background. Soon after, they hear the loud noise of her body landing on the bed. Claude begins to clean up the crumbs, silently winking at Sophie. Her bob is shorter than ever, her skinny jeans fitting loosely on her hips. The paperwork for Sophie to buy back Dean's share of the flat is being arranged. He is moving out this weekend. Sophie looks down at Claude, her blood boiling.

It takes resilience, she thinks, to love despite the disdain of others.

2

A friend of Sophie's recommended a small restaurant on top of a hill. The food is supposed to be *exquisite*, an adjective that makes Claude shrug when associated with the act of eating. Sophie books a table for eight o'clock and Giulia quickly checks her bank account balance on the tram. It becomes irrelevant as they sit together at their table, pour vinho verde into their glasses and start to snack on olives. The food is deliciously oily, their laughter flying at high pitch. They crack the crab's shell, their forks bumping into one another as they take a second bite of bacalhau. They lick their fingers, dip bread into the sauce covering the sardines, thirsty for more salt. They share recollections of previous summers together faster than time threads new memories. It really is a good night, here in Lisbon, on the terrace of a restaurant, none of them working and all eating at the same pace.

Giulia stops the waiter and orders another bottle of wine, and then more bread. 'To scarpetta,' she adds to Claude and Sophie, who have now learnt fragments of Italian through her. Not enough to be used properly but enough to feel close to their friend. Along the years, there are the odd words that have become part of their friendship's linguistics because they define Giulia. Tisana, madonna, esatto. Trivial words to them, yet a vocabulary that means the world to Giulia. They laugh further and faster, pour more wine, red this time, and Claude asks the waiter for his advice on what to order for dessert.

'Queijadas de requeijão de Évora,' he assures them.

'I think I read queijada comes from Sintra?' continues Giulia, who is often more curious about where her food is from than how it may taste.

Sophie has withdrawn from the conversation, sipping the last drops of wine.

The waiter smiles at Giulia before he continues, 'They are famous in Sintra, yes. Made of cheese, eggs, milk and sugar.'

'Requeijão seems similar to ricotta,' adds Claude.

'It is. But the one we have here is from Évora. Have you been down south yet?'

Sophie develops an urgent need to justify their plans. 'I'm afraid not. We only have time for Lisbon this time around.'

The waiter's smile widens before he adds, 'You should next time. In any case, the queijadas de requeijão is a small, sweet tart made of cheese. Sheep's cheese. We serve it with fresh strawberries. Should I bring three of them for you ladies?'

'That would be great. Thank you,' replies Claude.

'And three shots of Ginja,' adds Sophie nonchalantly. She has never worked in hospitality.

Claude and Giulia smile at the waiter as they hand back the dessert menus.

As they wait for tonight's final dish, Claude runs downstairs to the bathroom. She comes back to find that the night has turned political, a recurring problem with that final glass of the evening. She quietly sits back, listening to her friends arguing about why Brexit happened, picking up her phone and making a note to begin the paperwork for her French passport as soon they arrive back in London.

'How can you be defending a referendum that is threatening your right to live in London?'

'The fact that you're saying London and not the United Kingdom is part of the problem in itself. It's not the referendum that's the problem. It's the class system.'

'Juddy, please. Don't give me that old communist line.'

Claude jumps on this opportunity to put their argument to bed, 'You both read the *Guardian* every week. Neither one of you is a communist.' Her eyes bounce back and forth between both sides of the court. She pauses, smiles and restarts: 'I think I spotted our desserts on my way back.'

Sophie continues, 'You cannot dismiss the fact that in the end this country voted for Brexit. I'm not sure that's the kind of shared ownership you want, is it?'

'People voted for Brexit after a man promised them a referendum, so he would stay prime minister. If you're looking for figures to blame, blame the phalluses and leave the communists out of this one.'

'Your Corbyn boy was in favour of Brexit.'

'Was he?'

The waiter serves the desserts into a short stinging pause.

'If only you were able to see outside of your bubble, Soph.'

'You didn't complain about my bubble when I offered to pay more for the accommodation. Did you?'

Giulia's cheeks are redder than the leftover broken crab shell in front of her. 'You're paying more because you are the only one around this table who thinks it's worth it to pay an extra hundred quid so you can Instagram the bloody bathtub.' Their minds blur among the sound of other people's conversations.

'This pie is delicious. How interesting the flavour of sheep's milk is in this context. Can you taste it?' Claude shivers with embarrassment as soon as she asks, as soon as she notices that neither of her friend's spoons have brushed their plates yet. Do they think she is not capable of arguing about Brexit? She could if she wanted to, she does with Giulia when they settle into a safe conversation together, sharing opinions, challenging each other's point of view. Sophie downs her Ginja and goes to the bathroom. As soon as she disappears from their sight, Giulia devours her dessert. 'Don't you even try to defend her.'

'She's drunk. She will regret it tomorrow.'

Giulia could slam her fist against the table if she were not so afraid of anger. She longs to stand up, walk to the bathroom and pull Sophie's hair. To call Sophie out for not eating a bite tonight, at this restaurant she had chosen out of all the options they could have gone for, not a taste of the most expensive meal she could pick. And suddenly Giulia feels pathetic. She regrets having had this conversation with Sophie, or at least tonight, in the middle of a restaurant on holiday, after a stimulating amount of wine. She wants to speak honestly about money with her friend, this authoritative agency that frightens her, one that influences where she aligns herself on the worthy curve that bends between them. They have never attached the same value to wealth – what Sophie defines as *cheap* makes Giulia chuckle. But she has a fear of not being there for her friend because she simply cannot afford it. She must confess, not having to organise Sophie's hen do has come as a relief.

Sophie reappears, reapplying her lipstick. 'I paid the bill. Should we grab a last drink along the way?'

Giulia pours herself water, ice cubes falling heavy to the bottom of her glass.

'It's been a long day. Let's go home,' says Claude, nodding at Giulia in confidence.

3

Sophie is still fast asleep when Claude and Giulia bring back their cups of coffee to the sink. The forecast is already warm and they both feel sticky, their mouths furry from the wine they drank the night before. They remember the crab's claw and their stomachs rumble. The walls of the apartment have faded greyer overnight and Giulia has light purple rings under her eyes. Claude has not slept much either, not since Sophie knocked on her door around 3:30 in the morning because she could not sleep. She stroked her friend's hair until she fell back asleep. They didn't mention the episode in the restaurant. Sophie knows Claude would have stood up for Giulia. Claude washes the cups, Giulia dries them. They decide to go for a morning stroll; there is no knowing when Sophie might wake up.

'Don't hang on to what Sophie said yesterday.'

'I'm not.'

'You seem quiet, though.'

'Do you see the blue trousers hanging between the two windows over there?' Claude turns her head towards the cement walls that have been left bare, a rusty cord in between, blue worker's trousers hanging to dry. Giulia continues, 'Mum does the same thing. Every Saturday morning, she washes

75

the past week's worth of my stepdad's trousers. He is not allowed to bring them inside the house because they smell like the factory. All those chemical products they use. She makes him undress in the entrance and he leaves his trousers in a small sealed bag by the door, until she picks them all up first thing on Saturday morning, washes them, and then hangs them to dry outside our window.' Giulia gazes towards Claude. 'I used to feel such shame because of this.'

'From the trousers?'

'It was so obvious, you know, all of them at once, floating like flags. I saw them as proof that Paolo does not have a reason to wear any other clothes than the factory ones and that my mother washes them for him.'

'I find the blue of the trousers beautiful.'

Giulia smirks. 'It was one of my first cultural shocks. The cool kids in East London who wear working men's jackets to go to clubs.'

Claude giggles. Giulia begins to laugh too, but abruptly stops herself, looking ahead as they walk through the awakening city: 'It's not about what she said. I mean, it is true: she paid more for this holiday because I cannot afford it. It's just that I wonder how we can be so close when we seem incapable of understanding how the other sees the world.'

'You do.'

'We hurt each other's feelings all the time.'

'You are both envious of the other's life, that's all. You live so differently, like a broken mirror of one another. At the end of the day you love each other. That's what matters.'

'I don't know, Claude. I don't think I see Sophie the way you do.'

Claude shivers, suddenly aware of the drips of sweat rolling down her forehead.

'How do you see Sophie?'

'Honestly, Claude? Toxic. Don't get me wrong, I love her, I really do. But somehow she hurts me each time I try to share something more intimate with her. This lack of empathy when I feel so much. Maybe I'm asking too much from her and our friendship.'

'I'm sorry, Giulia. I don't think it's about you, it's about her own insecurities.'

'It's not you who should be apologising. Do you think she has asked me about Teddy since we arrived?'

'She's mourning Dean. How is Teddy?'

Giulia stops. Here, in the middle of the pavement, despite the pedestrians going ahead with their errands, Giulia has stopped. 'Why do you always defend her?'

'I'm not. Quite the opposite. I'm trying to walk away from the discord. Don't put me in the middle, please, Giulia.'

'Clearly I cannot read either of you these days. Perhaps I'm the one who lacks empathy.'

Claude gently runs her right hand down her friend's arm and they continue to walk. Giulia shares new information about Teddy, about how she surprises herself thinking that she might love him, especially when she wakes up in the morning. Does Claude think this is a good sign? Teddy is doing well with his job so his visa is secured in that sense, but she is worried he might want to go back to Australia at some point. 'You know, his family is there. And it's so much warmer,' she explains, shyly. She wouldn't want to move all the way to Australia. Her family wouldn't let her, she brushes this off with a swift laugh.

They soon find their way back to the apartment, pastéis de nata in hand. They set up the small table on the balcony, another pot of coffee on the way, the pastries nicely arranged on a plate. Claude slides the bedroom door open so the light is allowed inside and invites Sophie to jump out of bed. A few minutes later, she joins them, still in her pyjamas shorts, her hair flat at the back of her head, her mascara from the night before running down her cheeks. She rubs her eyes, noticing the black ink on her fingers, and suddenly she looks faint to her friends. Giulia invites her to sit with them.

'Good morning, sleepy beast,' adds Claude.

Sophie lets a light smile sculpt her face and plunges into one of the plastic chairs. She is now yawning loudly as she takes a photo of the breakfast table. Claude and Giulia eye one another.

'How are you feeling, Sophie?' asks Claude.

'A little rough, but this looks delicious,' she adds, while cringing at Giulia who is licking her finger after she wolfed down a pastel.

Giulia picks up another, 'These *are* delicious.'

'We bought an assortment. Some are plain, others have raspberries, coconut, I think. Maybe vanilla? Or is that the classic one?'

'What time did you wake up?' Sophie interrupts, worried she might have missed an important event, something they might refer to again later in life. She wants to be featured on the holiday photos; she wants to be able to say she was there and to heartily laugh at the memories next time they meet.

'Sometime around nine, I think.'

Giulia is typing away on her phone. Claude attempts to call a ceasefire between her friends: 'How is Teddy this morning?'

Sophie gets up and comes back with a glass of water for herself. She turns her phone screen up and smiles as her breakfast photo has already been liked a dozen times. She has not tried any of the pastries yet. 'What should we do today?'

Giulia responds first: 'I would love to walk to the Belém tower.'

'Happy with that. I only want to make sure I go to the artisan's market tomorrow morning,' Claude adds.

'Maybe we can end the day with one of those porto wine factory visits?'

Sophie's suggestion is received with a short silence.

'Sure, we should learn about porto wine,' concludes Claude.

'Well, I'd better go and shower.' Sophie runs to the bathroom and Claude is left with Giulia, who is staring at her phone. She turns her screen towards Claude, showing her Sophie's social media profile. Claude rolls her eyes and gets up to clear the plates. Giulia follows and puts Sophie's untouched plate straight back on the shelf.

'Efficient,' she adds as she tenderly taps Claude's shoulder. 'I'll brush my teeth. Let's go get some sun.'

They head out and start to walk. They stop a few times so Claude can add another layer of sunscreen. Sophie buys a pack of cigarettes to share. Giulia runs towards the water and dips her feet in the small rockpools while Claude and Sophie sit back on the riverside. She joins them a few minutes afterwards, pearls of water drifting down her calves. She tells them about the first time she drove to the seaside with her mother. She was seven years old, or perhaps eight, but that's not relevant. It was the first time her mother told her about how she moved to Italy – she had not realised before that day that Marija, her mother, might be from a different country than her. It was the two of them, plus her baby stepbrother Alessandro, as her stepfather took on another shift during his supposed holidays. Giulia smiles at the recollection of the open windows and of her mother singing all the way to La Spezia, where a family friend owned a small hotel. Marija helped in the laundry room in the mornings so they could stay in one of the spare rooms for free. It was the first time Giulia understood her mother also had a mother. That she must miss her. Giulia slides her tongue over her lips before she tells her friends about all the different kinds of focaccia she tried over the course of this holiday, for breakfast, lunch and dinner. Sophie almost apologises for yesterday night but she decides otherwise. They are happy now. They walk for another short while, until they stop for lunch.

When the pavement narrows down, it is Giulia who steps back so Sophie and Claude can move forward together.

4

They stop for coffee somewhere. Claude and Giulia are vigorously listing what they enjoy about Lisbon: the red of the walls, the tiles, the graffiti, the kiosks, the specialist shops – they passed a shop dedicated to wooden stamps earlier today – the church's bell tower. Their voices meld with the surrounding chatter and the ambient racket of a European city, which is also something they list. Giulia vividly approves of the noise of the city, the narrow streets coming alive and reinvigorating years of time passing, lives fading, walking through a place where history grips onto every single stone of the roads and buildings.

'It really makes me feel alive,' Claude concludes. They are silent now. Claude rests her eyes in the sun and Giulia observes, her legs up on the chair's armrest. Sophie drops her phone loudly against the metallic table.

'Bad news, though, we should be in Porto, really, if we want to visit a port house.' Her two friends already knew this, although they don't have the heart to tell Sophie. 'But I booked us in for a wine tasting at the Lisbon Winery. They offer a *typical tasting experience, paired with local charcuterie and cheese.*'

'What time have you booked for?'

'Seven.'

'Should we have dinner afterwards, then?'

Claude leans back on the chair, resting her eyes further, as Giulia and Sophie continue to debate over dinner. Will a plate of charcuterie and cheese be enough? Should they already book somewhere else? It is brilliant that booking a table at a restaurant in Europe is only one phone call away: no website, no newsletter to subscribe to, no credit card details to put down to secure your booking. Sophie wants to go dancing later tonight and they don't want to feel bloated. 'Fair enough,' continues Giulia, but they also don't want to drink all night on an empty stomach. Claude is nodding in the background, grateful she remembered to grab her sunglasses as they stepped out earlier. They are now reviewing what they should wear, Sophie increasingly flustered: they must pay fast so they will have time to go back to the apartment and get changed. More chatter; no, Giulia does not want Sophie to lend her a dress, she brought one, actually.

'Claude, do you remember the green one we bought together a few weeks ago?'

Claude steps away from her chair. 'Yes, lovely dress. Should we take the tram?'

'Yes. What will you wear, Claude?'

'Claude will wear her yellow polka dot dress. You're sun-kissed already, Clo, you will look delicious.'

Blushing, Claude shivers. 'I did bring it. OK, let's go home so I can wash my hair.'

'Now I'm excited.' Giulia punctuates this with a rapid side jump, and the three friends walk faster than they did when they first left the apartment that morning.

When they reach the wine bar, they all wear lipstick. Even Claude was convinced. 'The orangey tone will look so beautiful against the yellow of your dress,' Giulia had reassured her while Sophie applied the colour. She is happy that it covers the mole she finds unattractive on her upper lip but she finds it foolish to wear lipstick when they are about to taste wine. The lip marks on the glasses will trigger a bitter taste in her mouth: those small stains of insecurity. She hates them.

'It's a reliable lipstick. You'll be fine. You look pretty, Clo,' Sophie said as she finished her friend's make-up. Since the first time she saw her toying with textures and colours, Claude has thought Sophie looks her sharpest when she applies make-up. She follows the same procedure each time, her eyes and mind in control as she thinks fast in response to the other's skin tone and features, her fingers sliding over the various tools she requires. First, she hydrates Claude's skin with hyaluronic acid and a moisturising cream from one of the luxurious pastel-coloured pots. She then applies a foundation, mixed together with a prep cream, conscious that Claude's skin is on the edge of crumbling, her index finger circling against her palm as she mixes the two products until she obtains the wanted shade, her eyes frowning, showing off her left dimple. *So it holds together*, she mutters slowly as her fingers brush against Claude's maxillae. Sophie's hands then start to move faster, aligning Claude's expression, instructing her to turn her profile right and left, to close and open her mouth and eyes. A concealer under Claude's eyes, a fixing translucent powder, and she is now ready to begin her make-up. Looking into Clo's eyes, she blends a light nude eyeshadow and signs it off with a slim line of eyeliner. She stops the line before the end of each eye – ever since Claude instructed her not to draw all the way along, as it accentuates how round her eyes appear, she had explained, looking at her toes. Sophie adds a touch of highlight in the middle of the eyelid instead, which makes her eyes spark, echoing today's sunlight and the piercing glow it has given to Claude's pupils. She moves on to brushing the brows, grinning as she does: Sophie adores Claude's bushy eyebrows. She never applies lacquer on them, quite the opposite; she plays with their movement and length. Sophie steps back, her hands resting on both sides of Claude's face, her gaze undisturbed, focused. *Fab*, she exhales, as she grabs a fluffy brush and begins to apply darker shadows on Claude's cheekbones, with a final touch of blush in the exact spot where her cheek is at its highest when she smiles. Sophie's lips are pressed tight again, a sign of her concentrating. Claude can feel Sophie's warm breath against her own mouth at this point. Sophie's eyes are settling on Claude's lashes as she applies mascara in thick layers, the extra black and volume edition. As if she can sense the mounting heat, Sophie abruptly instructs Claude to open her mouth, and applies a nude lip balm. Finally, she adds the colourful lipstick.

Tonight, in Lisbon, Sophie opted for a light shade of orange before she stepped back, a bright smile illuminating her creation as Claude shyly grinned back before she rose and turned to face the mirror. She felt pretty, a pleasant realisation that swiftly dissolved with the acknowledgement that she did not recognise herself. The pretty face in the mirror, the glossy cheeks and popping lips, did not resemble hers but instead emerged as an insight into her failure to be part of her crew of girlfriends, these two beautiful women. She stepped backwards, her back against the wall, her palms pressed against the chilled bathroom mosaics. Sophie was rolling her fingers across the pens and tubes from her beauty case, making small scratching noises. The light appeared brighter suddenly. Giulia shook a bottle until she started dispensing what looked like whipped cream to Claude, which alerted her to how disconnected she was from this room and reminded her how estranged she often feels from the girls and their rituals.

Sophie turned around, exclaiming, 'I love the curls!'

Giulia was staring back at the projection of herself in the mirror, a closed-mouth smile broadening her cheeks. She did look beautiful tonight.

The waiter is wearing a suit and sprinkles his discourse with more *ladies* than they need to feel important. They settle downstairs, where the walls are raw stone, among the beautiful wooden barrels. It is chilly and they regret not bringing a shawl with them, except Claude, who did. It is lovely here, she thinks. It reminds her of the storage room at the café, easing her mood, making her feel at home again. The waiter begins to list the tastings they offer, starting with the deluxe option before he upgrades to the premium service. He is working on the assumption that they already thought the deluxe experience sounded *terrific.* They should hear about what else he can offer them. Do they know about the traditional method that is used to open port bottles? For an extra ninety euros, they will have the same amount of port wine but it will be served from vintage bottles, and opened through heating the stem.

'Let's go premium,' says Giulia first. Her friends hide their surprised looks, staring at the waiter, long neck and a faint smile for armour.

'Great, I will introduce you to Ruben, who is going to serve you tonight.'

'Well, for that price, let's hope Ruben is hot,' says Sophie as soon as the waiter is gone, louder than Claude wishes.

They laugh.

They drink all five sorts of port and order an extra bottle of Dão white wine. The crispness is quickly making their heads buzz. Tonight, the conversations are turned towards others, commenting on the last time they saw Jane and how uptight she looked, feeling sorry for Nathan, gossiping about who among their old friends had gotten married, so they heard or guessed from their social media, reviewing everyone's career path in comparison to expired ambitions from their university days, agreeing how cute Candice's baby is, finally sending a photo of the three of them together to Nick. It is better this way. They are on their second night, there is nothing new to say. They have turned into lighter versions of themselves – less politicised, less angry, less joyful too – with the small but heavy layer of dread alcohol has added to their brains. They tip Ruben more than they would have for lunch but they did have a good night. When they emerge back upstairs, the sun has been replaced by thick air, brought by the night after a long and warm day. Various music tempos bang against one another, echoing through their boozy heads and empty stomachs. They stop by the bathroom on their way out, touching up their lipstick, checking where to head next.

'Bless *Time Out*,' Sophie declares as she scrolls through the blog in the background.

Giulia mumbles something unintelligible as she applies mascara. Claude translates, 'She is wondering about food.'

Sophie snorts but does not reply. 'No,' Giulia continues, 'I was saying that a friend told me about this bar on top of a car park. We should go there for a drink.'

'Where is that, then?'

A woman enters the bathroom and casts her eyes at the ground straight away, apologising for intruding. Claude is surprised by another wave of heat hitting her body.

'Let's move. We will find somewhere to go dancing for sure.'

'Bless the continent!' Giulia adds as she slams the bathroom door behind them.

They never found the bar on top of the car park but it is for the best in the end. What they enjoy the most is drinking on the pavement, smoking cigarettes, going back inside for another drink along with a quick dance, embraced by the sound of a familiar rhythm. As the night continues, they begin to sit more often than they stand, but still on the pavement. They chat, they laugh, they scream. They drink from plastic cups, Claude briefly mentions how bad for the environment this night out is, consuming a new plastic cup each time, throwing their cigarette butts on the ground. The girls roll their eyes and Claude does not dare bring down the mood further. She does feel bad tonight though, a small pinch in her stomach is growing into a hole. *It's only hunger,* she murmurs to herself. She goes to the bathroom and breaks her strict rule against cystitis: she must sit and rest. When Claude comes back outside, she finds two men have paired up with Sophie and Giulia. They are from the Netherlands, also on a short holiday in Lisbon. The chatter grows louder and Claude's head is pounding faster than her heart. Arend and Chris have decided to stick to the trio and they know somewhere to dance. It turns out that Chris did his Erasmus in Lisbon a few years ago; Sophie is convinced this is a sign they must follow. Giulia really wants to dance. Claude likes the idea of not having to talk anymore. They hear the brouhaha from the street ahead of turning the final corner. They all walk fast, something between a blissful jog and a series of little jumps. Giulia reminds them to stop at the cash machine for the cover charge. They debate how much it might be at length before they decide to take out more money, *to be on the safe side*. Soon their wrists are stamped and they are allowed inside. The sticky floor is grounding them as they order more shots and as the music carries them away. They dance throughout the night, with the occasional nod and laughter to the other. The two Dutch men disappear when they realise the friends do not need them to have a good time. When Claude, Giulia and Sophie begin to dance together, there is no room left for ignoring their bond – they do not need to speak nor to look at one another to share the same pace.

When they exit the nightclub, Claude's dress is stained, Sophie is walking barefoot and Giulia's hair is tucked into a bun. The sun has begun to rise, the sky moving from shades of navy blue to vivid purple. Giulia still has energy to burn, Claude's senses are awakening as the Lisbon bakers' hands begin to roll pastries. They start to notice the basement kitchens; they are everywhere. Small windows at the height of their ankles, wide open, a delicious stream of butter and custard smell escaping. A new day has arrived and they still feel festive. Giulia eyes Claude, who turns towards Sophie, who is dragging her feet, heels in hands, head down.

'Should we run up the stairs?'

Claude doesn't have time to object before Giulia arrives

on the second set of steps. She looks back towards Sophie, who is falling behind, before she launches herself upwards. She cannot remember the last time her legs jumped ahead at such a pace; it is thrilling.

'Wait for me, Giulia,' she surprises herself by calling out.

They stop in between two sets of stairs to check on Sophie, who is waving her hands at them, allowing them to move forward, to chase the view. They have reached Bairro Alto. Claude and Giulia sit on top of the steps, Claude resting her head against Giulia's shoulder, a rare moment of intimacy that is welcomed with a short and peaceful silence. They can see Sophie again and begin to cheer for her, 'Come on, Soph! The view is beautiful here!'

'Run, Sophie, run! We're going to make it for sunrise,' encourages Giulia.

When Sophie finally reaches them, her body is shaking, gasping for oxygen. They walk a few more metres until they feel the wind hitting their faces – they have arrived at the top, only the void ahead, overlooking Lisbon. There is nothing else to say so they let their bodies give in to the benches. The sky is now stretching into a palette of orange and it won't be long until the first streams of sun appear. They must savour this moment before the sun reaches the top and attracts locals and tourists outside. Not a noise in the background, the bodily reassurance of their friends next to them, they contemplate the horizon. It is not mystic, they do not reconsider their life choices. They simply are content. Perhaps it is the nature of the decade they live in but they often fall, exhausted, from the peak of their emotions, from deep sadness to explosive happiness. They worry they might be what is called *unstable*, the hysteria of their generation. Secretly, they do envy the idea of a possible lightness of being, they contemplate boredom, a quiet flow of stable feelings running through their lives. They are dozing off, somewhere between their present thoughts and tomorrow's hangover. Giulia lets herself go, her body now stretched out on a bench, her two hands tucked behind her head for a cushion. In the background, the city begins to set in motion, the first workmen drilling, the odd car passing by. Even Claude and Giulia had not anticipated what happens next. The sudden loud burp, Sophie's legs rushing to the green recycling bin at the end of the esplanade, her vomiting out the past night. Claude follows her closely, holding her hair back into a ponytail, pushing her palm against her back, telling her to count to a hundred, all the way to 'cent'.

Giulia stays behind, refusing to step between the pair, her gaze still; clouds are appearing, drawing a curtain over this new day.

Giulia

In a stone house the air is kept cold. There aren't many windows and fewer doors. The coast is close enough that if you wake up earlier than your neighbours, you may hear the waves knocking on the rocks. In anticipation of when the first stream of light will flow through the house, waking up the men, the women tie their aprons around their waists, open cupboards, put pots of water to boil. Marija followed the same order of events every day, and so did every single woman she knew. *It isn't so bad*, she thought then. The dry land that surrounded the house was their curse. It gave Marija so much work in the house – *all the dust, you would not believe it*, she used to tell me, agitated in her apartment in Italy – it gave the elderly folks in the house a terrible cough, it produced no vegetables to sell. When he came home with empty hands, he was to be feared. But Marija knew better. Violent men are gospel truth to her and though her mother did not know how to read she had taught her how to defeat the beast. She bought the small pills from another woman, who travelled to the city once a month with the village's church committee. While the men had their eyes closed, at sermon time, she acquired the pills with a tight smile. Supplies would then follow – cheese, rosemary, tangerines – later during the week, as compensation. While he was out, and that was most days except Saturdays, Marija crushed the pills in her mortar into a fine white powder, and then poured it into the wine she was not allowed to drink. It dissolved instantly. He was asleep before nine o'clock every day, except Saturdays. *Because your father worked so hard*, Marija would explain, another kind of tight smile lighting up her face. I admire my mother's beauty – the coarseness of her features; square jaw and thick, dark hair.

In the family portrait I have crafted, a mixture of my mother's memory and the vivid present picture I have of her, Marija was bewitched by the year of 1989. The Velvet Revolution in the Czech Republic, the protests in Hungary, the fall of the Berlin Wall, borders reopening, people moving back to their mother countries, those who went on to build new homes. Marija herself wrote a different story, which she sealed on the day her passport was stamped: 'Giulia, cara, I could not have my daughter grow up with a drug addict for a father.'

My mother has the driest sense of humour and she refuses to say a word in Croatian. 'È una cosa che appartiene al passato, amore.'

I admire her strength. She does not need any help to

move the old leather sofa around the living room so she can follow the light while she sits, sewing metres of recycled fabrics into new items. The strength with which she kneads pizza dough. We had pizza every Sunday but we still went to church. When she married Paolo, it was simple enough to hide the certificates from her previous *foreign* marriage. I don't think Nonna knows my mother's story and I often wonder if she realises she was not born in Italy. There are wrinkles of such a knowledge in both their voices – Marija's odd accent from time to time; Nonna's rare and sharp defensiveness – but these are the things we don't talk about. Paolo and Marija met outside a café: he was on his way to the factory and she was gasping for new air, inhaling the urban expressions around her. She was holding a cup of coffee while slowly swaying her hips to the rhythm of the ambient Bolognese music – cars, quarrels, whistles; all new sounds to her. Paolo stopped in front of Marija, suddenly, intrigued, and asked what music she was dancing to. My mother, who was still shy about her Italian then, moved her arms in circles around her face, 'la città, ascolta la città.' *Listen to the city*. I don't know anything else about the early years of Paolo and Marija, not until the day they said *yes* to each other in a quiet church, with me, baby Alessandro and Nonna for witnesses. All I know is that when she quietly pointed to the Moses basket on the chair behind her outside that café, Paolo's face lit up at the sight of mine.

My mother hasn't stopped dancing since. Marija was surprised when she first crossed the border, her radio switching to RAI, the Radio Audizioni Italiane then, to hear music she did not expect. Where had *La Traviata* and the political songs gone? As she began to understand the lyrics, her curiosity for Italy grew, this country she now calls home. We still play the rapper Jovanotti in our home, Paolo and Nonna frowning so hard their thick eyebrows cover most of their faces, Marija boisterously singing until she stops, looks at us and adds: 'Jovanotti taught me Italian, we owe him one song.' It was the first music she heard on the radio, that day in November 1989. She is loyal, Marija.

The only time I saw Marija cry was on the day of my First Communion. I had just come home, dressed in a white gown, proud that I had been granted the right to share the body of Christ. I was one of the grown-ups now, sitting at the table, a piece of Nonna's torta tenerina before me, looking at my mother who was gazing outside through the window. It started as a small, uneasy feeling. I was almost done with my slice of cake and she had not even taken a bite of hers. The distance I felt from her as her eyes ran away through that window; was I not the star of the day after all? She was not there, the mother who had never failed to witness each one of my life events, the mother who always made me believe my world could be bigger than hers. Why was she refusing to share this moment with me? I quietly followed the tear running down her cheek. One single tear, until she looked at me and said, 'Never forget that it is the women in your family who have your back, not the Lord.'

Paolo worked in a factory. It was not good for his back but he was content with his timetable and they had a good workers' union. He spent long hours at the bar. Marija took care of the house and ironed for the extra cash. Each one of those shirts brought smiles to my face; from a cornetto on the way to school to my first minidress, and finally to the violin I will carry years later in a second cabin bag on my flight to London. It surprises people who don't know me well that I play the violin. *Lively, exuberant Giulia who runs marathons and loves electronic music.* I, Giulia, can lose track of the hours as I play the same tune again and again. I am not interested in playing for anyone other than for my family. That is most certainly why I never went on to become the brilliant violinist Paolo, Marija and Nonna thought I had the potential to be. Paolo dramatically tossed the artificial flowers – which usually reigned on the console table in the entrance of our apartment – to me after each one of my performances. Marija clapped her hands loudly, shouting celebratory comments just as dramatically. Nonna pretended she was not crying. I bring my violin with me each time I go back to Italy, even if I am only there for a weekend.

I went to university in Bologna. Between my shifts at a local restaurant where menus were available in English and my childhood bedroom, education became a serious option for me. I was proud of this. I was the first one to go to university, across both sides of the family, and I will spare you the tale of my graduation party. All you need to know is that not even Sophia Loren would have received a more decadent celebration if she had ever graced our front door. Within a week, I was on my way to the airport for my move to London: there was no job for me in Bologna. My announcement was received with quiet nods and an extra portion of ragù from Nonna. I think my mother knew better than to comment on the circle of life. She drove me to the airport alone. She did not leave her car, *kiss and fly*, we never were huggers. I paused before I unlocked the door.

'Thank the Lord you can run away by plane and with the air con on these days,' she said, her eyes looking ahead. I kissed her on the right cheek and opened the door.

I had a grand plan to move somewhere called the United Kingdom. Regno Unito: the fifth ranked economy in the world, a country where hard work leads to a secure job, a community where it's acceptable for women to drink as much as men, the culture that produced the Beatles, the Cure, the Rolling Stones. As simple as that. I got off the plane and made my way to Liverpool Street Station. There it struck me: how can so many people need to be in the same place at the same time? The brutal realisation that I am not only my mother's daughter but one inconsequential person among a crowd, and that there is no going home tonight. The English of the other train passengers carried various turns of tongue and musicality, but their voices were different from the ones I had heard before. Why did I not seem to understand simple words anymore? I needed to build a new home first. I am still building a home, stepping away from this rabbit hole of needs we dig for ourselves. You must see this and do that and go there and don't forget to post a picture of it on your social media. What is this or that; where is there; what am I taking a picture of? *Una mattina mi son svegliato*, the song begins. The constant pressuring questions that drive me forward during the day, shelved under the dirty word 'capitalism' at night. *Una mattina mi son svegliato / e ho trovato l'invasor.* Paolo, who spent hours at the café with his co-workers, glorifying socialism, strengthens my muscles. The songs from the crowds marching through the ever-protesting Bologna chant in my head. *O bella ciao, bella ciao, bella ciao ciao ciao.* It makes me angry that I still barely can make ends meet despite having stopped counting my extra hours, admin tasks mainly, marketing products I would never find a use for, sailing further away from the music industry that brought me here in the first instance. *So much bureaucracy in Italy, it's insane*, my colleagues often remind me. *O partigiano portami via / ché mi sento di morir.* I still haven't set a foot in most of my friends' houses and what is it with jacket potatoes? I queue. I queue a lot: online to buy a ticket, at venues, at restaurants. The coffee is weak. But I call London home. I have dug my own hole. *O bella ciao, bella ciao, bella ciao ciao ciao.*

Nonna sends me boxes of mortadella and parmigiano in the post. I rarely see the bottom of my shelf before I receive the next package. These are some of my favourite days in London, when my old home travels to my new one, when I feel in two places at once. I adore that in London the buildings are short, that I could dance any day of the week if I wanted to, the vivid burgundy of the bricks when the sun goes down. The corner shops remind me of the small grocery stores I go to back in Italy. I do struggle to figure out where most of the produce comes from, though. Is that too much to ask – perhaps we do not have time in London to consider where our tangerines should come from? The strawberries are British, this much I know. I have run this city up and down multiple times. I wasn't athletic before I moved here; this is an addition, my London-Giulia-self, if I may. The pace of life is so fast; I had to build better endurance, so I started going on runs. The truth is that I struggled to make friends and running a half-marathon will take the day away from you: warming up, running it, cooling down and recovering lying down flat on the floor in the corridor, legs up against the wall. I mean, I met people, quickly, many of them. Life is a constant stream of people but I speak to less than one per cent of them. And then, those I speak to, well, you know, it takes time to have the friends you want to have and not the ones you must go along with because life presented them to you and you quite like to socialise at the end of the day. It took time but then they appeared, as I danced, like Marija did years before in Bologna. Then I did what my mother told me to do; I found my women: Claude and Sophie.

Still Summer

1

Sophie walks straight to the bathroom, losing one item of clothing after each step. Claude is already running a cold bath. Giulia had decided to stay on her bench on top of Bairro Alto.

'The green is the same colour as the cedars from the Giardini Margherita in Bologna. I'll stay here a little longer,' she had announced, eyes firmly closed.

Sophie plunges under the water, her head pounding, chills disrupting her body. When she resurfaces, Claude is the first thing she catches sight of: monochrome, always dressed either in all black or yellow, consistently beside her. She sometimes wonders what the air would taste like if Claude was not breathing next to her. Would her cells dissolve? Would her lungs stop filtering carbon dioxide? Would the air turn toxic? She has always loved chemistry, she has a flair for it even

101

– Sophie can make the most vivid eyeshadows from the most unlikely substances – but the solubility of both their beings is one she cannot solve. *I must do this now or I will never do it.* She stares into Claude's eyes, sitting in the bathtub, knees up with her chin resting on them, eyes still while her body shakes from the hangover. Alcohol pearls down her back and melts into the cold water.

Claude kneels down, gently running the tips of her fingers through the water. 'We used to do this with my mother.'

'Get smashed?' Sophie says.

Lines of dripping, steamy water imitate tears on the mirror behind them.

'Bathe. Well, I bathed and she sat on the floor next to the bathtub. She was always topless, she explained it was to avoid getting wet when rinsing my hair. Although she always said that a woman should not be obliged to cover her tits. Look at me, I did not inherit my mother's exuberance, eh?' Claude's hands pre-empt her brain as she tucks Sophie's hair back behind her left ear.

'I wish I knew her.'

'And I wish she knew you.' They pause. 'The bath ritual, it was a Sunday thing. She would read Jack London's *The Call of the Wild* to me out loud. The state of that book, doubled in size from the damp, you wouldn't believe it. But I loved that dog. Buck.' Claude is smiling now, her eyes rolling upwards, searching for the sound of Maman's voice. Sophie's teeth chatter in the background. 'Let's get you out of there.' And as she opens a towel for Sophie, she continues: 'I started to call my mother a she-sled-dog. I was unaware it was not grammatically correct then, and that there was simply not a female form of "sled dog". Maman never corrected me. It was our English teacher who did. At school, in front of the entire class, and everyone laughed. Do you remember?'

Sophie turns around, wrapped in the towel, finding Claude again: 'I didn't laugh.'

There is another pause. Claude makes to step away but Sophie grapples quickly for her hand and holds tight. They lock eyes, each desperately seeking assurance in the other's expression. The gurgle of draining water echoes on the bathroom tiles, then silence. Sophie's towel drops. Claude steps towards Sophie's lips, blue from the cold bath, squeezing her shaking hand. They kiss.

Years of giggles, fights, pep talks, tears, disappointments, laughter, silent nods, feeling alive next to one another, glances from opposite corners of each room they walked through, years of emotions suddenly distilled into one small act of tenderness, both delicious and frightening. Will they look the same once their lips separate and their eyes meet again? Everything and nothing has been shared between Claude and Sophie. But there is one thing they have always safeguarded from one another – and that is the taste of their bodies. This was, until now, reserved for their other partners, who needed to feel they owned something of Sophie or Claude that the other could not share.

The pace is slow at first; delaying climax for as long as it can be bearable for their bodies. It is sour and salty and liberating. What might come after has a threatening bittersweet taste attached, a soft ending or a romantic beginning. Either way, they are turning a corner. Fingers running down hips, Sophie's hair dripping water on their stomachs, Claude's tongue growing confident. They do not speak, until Sophie begs Claude to move faster, until she asks Claude to turn around and finally feels capable to give her friend the reassurance she has always been given through everyday acts of kindness. It is not about listening to one another; it is about anticipation and execution. They are exploring their desires, though hasty to acknowledge how they might hurt the other. It tastes new, this ability to exist wholly, bodily and emotionally, alongside one another. Breaths shorten as they commit to find what the other might want or need to hear and feel – legs widening, voices unleashed in emancipation. Their bodies release.

Afterwards they remain silent, their backs cooling down against the cold floor of the bathroom. Claude can smell the bleach from the cleaners' work this morning and Sophie licks her lips, in search of Claude's chemical property. Their feet shyly brushing, they both picture their dream of a house in Provence. The lavender will be buzzing with bees and bed sheets will be put out to dry on the line in the garden, where the green will extend far away. They will grow olives and lemons; Claude will make tapenade and tarts. On the front of the stone-walled house, there will be a rustic wooden table, with benches on both sides. They won't be good for their backs but they are more convivial: nobody will be allowed to leave the table until the last bite of melon, the last grilled sardine, the last scoop of salade niçoise has been eaten, except to refill the bread basket or pick up another bottle of rosé wine. À la bonne franquette. The kitchen will be painted in yellow as soon as they move in. They will interpret the white-checked flooring as a sign that cannot be unseen. At least, this is what they will tell Giulia before they explain that they are moving there for good. Giulia and Teddy, Nick, Hana, Candice, even Nathan and Jane, will visit them often throughout the year, more frequently from the first May bank holiday onwards. It will be a mystery to anyone how they live and what they do with their days, and they will not care since they will all inherit a free holiday house with this agreement. Nobody will dare to question what they do. What they do to one another. The bathroom floor remains ice-cold for now. Claude stands and Sophie sits up. She is looking at the bathtub, the small puddle of water at the bottom, cold foam crackling. She hesitates. She would like to say something but words fail her – if she were brave enough, she would turn back and hug her friend tightly.

Claude closes the door softly behind her.

2

Sophie climbs back into the bathtub. She plunges underwater, hair glued to her face, painful lungs running out of oxygen. She is running out of breath; she feels stiffer, tired, exposed.

Sophie resists, underwater, counting all the way to one hundred. She does not feel like she is drowning anymore, now that she is here. She is in control, her lungs not begging so powerfully for air anymore. She screams loudly and louder, still underwater.

One hundred.

Sophie resurfaces and buries her face inside a towel. She hates the lack of smell of holiday let towels. It is so impersonal to dry your body into a piece of laundry that has been shared by so many people it has lost its fragrance. Those worn-out towels, from the blending of everyone's habits and bodies and expectations, make Sophie sad. Her stomach pinches, an attempt to hold on to the hole from the meals she makes herself miss. The control she craves more than her appetite does, the flavours from the food challenge her barriers, her fork pushing bits into corners, mashing chunks into smaller and more malleable extracts. Sophie looks back at her reflection in the mirror, her make-up drifting down her face, her hair tangled and dripping, a small bruise on her arm appearing, the freckles the sun brought to her nose.

Fuck. The floor underneath her feels faint, her ankles hard–
ening. The vertigo from these few minutes hits her harder
than any of the hangovers her body has recovered from
before today, than any of the pain she has put herself through.
It was only a few seconds ago that her skin felt soft and
touched. She had hoped that with Claude it would feel
different, during and afterwards. Afterwards, especially.

Sophie grabs the small scissors in her beauty case and
begins to cut her nails short enough that vivid red blood
cracks through her skin. Fissures unstitch. Her feet keep her
steady on the ground as she continues to cut and then polish
her work with the help of a nail file, abruptly scratching her
flaking nails, her mind focused under the bathroom's blinding
neon light. Scratching. Scratching. Scratching little noises
before her.

Sophie scrapes until her bleeding fingers become numb,
until they stop begging her brain for touch.

3

Claude and Giulia are sipping coffee on the balcony when Sophie emerges through her bedroom doorframe, her hair tied up in a towel. She sits and pours herself a large mug of coffee.

'Girls, do we agree that after this holiday none of us will ever wear a bra again?'

Sophie coughs.

Claude smiles at Giulia, 'Not that I wear one most days.'

Sophie coughs again. When Claude pats her back, she shakes and jumps to the sink to pour herself a pint of water. The day is bright and brilliant but they feel achy from the night before, from transgressing in drinking, dancing and loving. They review their plan to visit the city's artisan market and hidden streets; they will go to the beach instead. Giulia does a quick search and discovers that the Praia de Carcavelos is only thirty minutes away on the train from Lisbon central.

'That sounds wonderful,' Claude agrees.

They grab their tote bags and make their way to the seaside.

The salt on her lips is disturbing Sophie. She can taste it, constantly; dry lips, scratching salt. She refuses to bathe. She won't surrender to the water, not twice in the same day.

Giulia is running wild on the sand, chatting with random people and Claude surprises herself by feeling envious of Giulia, this ability of hers to simply converse. She wishes she knew what to say to strangers – perhaps she would discuss the chances of encountering a jellyfish today, share an episode of having to wee on someone's arm to cure a sting. But all she can think about is Sophie's body, the lines that go down her back, tied together by a few freckles along the way. The feeling of bravery and shyness that cohabit in her stomach. This new type of hunger, a tingling little hunger. Does Sophie think about her body the same way? Is she repulsed by their fluids coming together?

'Have you ever been stung by a jellyfish, Claude?' Giulia interrupts, wanting to bring her introverted friend into the conversation.

'I haven't.' A short silence falls before Claude smiles at the strangers, sand sieving through her fingers, 'but I do remember the fear I had of them as a child. I was too afraid to put a toe in the sea, frightened by the image of Medusa. Méduse means jellyfish in French. Now I think she is an individualist.'

'I was so scared of her too,' adds one of the men in the group who are sat around a navy beach towel.

'Well, you had reasons to be. I'm part of her crew, I realised recently,' Claude replies.

The other men begin to play cards and Giulia steps away swiftly.

'I can't compete with that. What's your name?'

'Claude. You?'

'Josh. Where are you from?'

'I was born in Croydon.' She pre-empts the question: 'My mum is French. From Brittany, to be specific, hence the name and the fear of Medusa.' Claude looks away, towards the ocean.

'I like it,' he says, and so Claude's eyes return and they continue to talk. Sophie pretends she is asleep, sheltered on her oversized yellow towel, yesterday's sickness a convenient excuse, Claude's laugh in interludes between Josh's jokes for nightmares.

Giulia returns, her hair wet and knotted, and whispers into Sophie's ear: 'These two are getting on like a burning house!'

'Like a house on fire, Giulia.'

Giulia steps back. This sharp attack, as if a steel ruler had been snapped against the top of her fingers. Why does it matter suddenly if she does not speak proper English? How would they have done at the train station earlier without Giulia's basic knowledge of Portuguese? She thought her friends liked her remastered idioms, the sound of her rolling tongue, the pace of her English, her intimate language from somewhere between Bologna and London. Sophie, who has always been so loud about Brexit, her dream to remain and secure her freeing passport, fails to make her friend feel safe today. She wants to respond but does not feel entitled to do so, not anymore. She will use the power of silence instead, turning her back to Sophie and towards the sun the way lost children on the beach do. She joins Claude and Josh again, and makes a point of roaring with laughter for the rest of the afternoon.

They ride the train back to Lisbon, their final holiday evening stretching ahead of them. Their bodies are washed out from the sea air they are not used to; their minds shelter in a tender blur. They will soon reach the city again and their escape will come to an end. They will return to their jobs, the commute and their bank balances. Claude will cycle everywhere, short on cash after the holiday, and anxious about finding herself trapped on the Tube. Giulia is starting a new job in a few weeks' time, still marketing products she despises, but it came with a pay rise she has decided not to disclose to her friends, nor Teddy. Sophie is selling her flat, not yet sure where to move next. Dean has finished packing back in London. They are already worried at the thought of having to set up regular dates to see one another, finding a balance between their work life, respective friendships and finding time for both trio and duet time. Even after years of friendship they are still afraid to tell the one left out when they do something as a pair. A threesome always leaves one's soul feeling less loved, a bitter comparison. Claude, Giulia and Sophie each feel this sharp pain simultaneously, and alone, the most frequently. They know the pace of normal life will welcome them as soon as they set foot in London.

'What shall we do tonight?' And so, Giulia brings them back to the present tense. They must enjoy their last evening.

Sophie is drinking a Sagres straight from the bottle: 'I'm still feeling a little rough from yesterday. I wouldn't mind staying home.'

'What if we stop at the nice shop near our apartment and buy some fresh seafood?'

Giulia's smile widens, 'Sì! I love the sound of this. I think I might even be strong enough for wine by then.'

'Moi aussi. I hope they have prawns.'

'And crab!'

'I really fancy some octopus. Let me check if there is another shop, other than the one around the corner, so we can buy nicer and fresher products.' Sophie's tongue trips over the word *fresh*. 'We might even be able to grab a few bits to bring back home.'

Claude and Giulia nod in approbation and Sophie begins her research, mumbling along the way. *Seafood Lisbon. Best supermarket Lisbon. Where to do your shopping in Lisbon. Ah, food shopping, that's what I mean.* She looks back up. 'At least we don't have to worry about how sustainable we are tonight, commuting by train, walking, shopping locally.'

Claude nods further in approval.

'But you have to acknowledge those oysters were something, no?' Giulia adds with a spark in her eyes.

Sophie is still staring at Claude. 'Come on, Clo, say it.'

'They were delicious.' She stops before she adds, displaying a tight-lipped smile, eyes rolling, 'But it is outrageous that you girls drove all the way to Whitstable for twelve oysters.'

'The things we do for you, eh,' says Giulia as she drops her head on top of Claude's shoulder. Sophie returns to scrolling down her screen, her fingers too shaky, she repeatedly opens the wrong link.

On the last evening of their summer holiday, Sophie is losing control, and even the icy feel of her beer is failing to help.

'Because I love you, Soph.'

'Pass me the can of chickpeas, please, Claude.'

'But will we speak about this once we've cooked all the chickpeas?'

Sophie grabs the can from Claude's hands as she scans the aisle warily, aware someone might be watching them. Her hands are soft, Claude remembers.

'I don't think there is anything else to discuss. We're going back to London tomorrow. It will all be OK then.'

'Do you mean we will carry on as we always did before?'

What has changed? Sophie does not understand Claude's sudden urgency to speak about something that has always existed between them both. They only acted upon the feelings they have always shared, surely. She does not think it is something to discuss in the middle of a supermarket, flickering neon light making them both look paler than they have ever been.

'There simply is nothing to add, Claude.'

Sophie walks towards the wine section. Claude switches her brain to operating mode: they will slow-cook the chickpeas in the water from the can but they need onion and lemon and cavolo nero, if they can find it. *If I feed them, I live. If I know what to feed them, they will eat. If we eat together, there will be a we. If we eat, we live together.* She picks the vegetables and heads towards the seafood counter next. She can see Giulia from afar, holding bread and cheese in her hands, moving her head slowly, her curious eyes reading the signs.

'Madonna. Claude, some of these fishes must be made of gold!'

Claude is next to her now. 'Yet they are feasting on the tonnes of plastic we discard in our oceans every day.'

'Someone's in a mood. What's up?'

'Probably sunstroke, that's all. What do you fancy?'

Claude normally adores shopping for seafood, the tentacles, the big eyes, she does not find them repulsive at all. She loves the thought of cleaning an octopus, cracking a crab's pincer, peeling shrimp; eating with her fingers, dipping the meat into mayonnaise, or simply squeezing a slice of lemon on top. Except today. Today, Claude is finding sea creatures unbearably sad. Naked on ice, they will soon be cooked alive. Gutted. Boiled. Grilled.

They walk back to the flat in silence. The air is still warm and turning stuffy, the heat of the day gathering as the light turns gloomier, increasing the pressure in their bodies. Sophie excuses herself: she wants to take a quick nap and shower before dinner. Claude is relieved, especially when Giulia approaches the sink, keenly, and asks if she can help: she wants to learn how to wash and peel and cook the seafood.

She has never done it. She only buys smoked salmon or fish in tins or eats it at a restaurant. Will they get sick? Claude looks at her, harbouring a comforting smile despite her sealed mouth: no, they won't get sick. They can do it together.

They often cook together. It is Giulia who spends the most time with Claude back in the yellow kitchen in Walthamstow. She had never spent as much time opening cupboards, sliding open drawers, sorting cutlery, chopping and peeling vegetables, before she moved to London and met Claude. The kitchen back home in Bologna is Marija and her grandmother's territory. She is eager to learn and to taste, and Claude loves this about her friend. She was shy at first, observing, while Claude outlined every step she took, giving her a reassuring wink as she added more pepper, ground nutmeg, until the time she handed her the spoon so Giulia could start with a simmering soup. Giulia learnt the vocabulary of kitchen utensils from Claude, yet despite everything, a colander will always be a *thingy*. They still argue about the words cafetière and Moka and chicory and endives. Giulia became acquainted with measurements, with combining spices and what they are called. She learnt that spices must be awakened to reach their highest flavour. She has taught Claude a few words of Italian in exchange, or corrected her usage of the singular and plural form for gnocchi for instance, as well as her pronunciation. The kitchen is always busy with the noise of spoons being slammed against pots in an attempt not to waste any of the tomato sauce, of their wine glasses knocking against the measuring cups, of eggs being broken, and above all, the air is filled with their laughter. They bring a part of their kitchen with them everywhere they go, the spiderweb they thread through their lives and fall back on at difficult times.

The kitchen in their holiday accommodation has finally turned yellow, the sun plays hide-and-seek with Lisbon and the day draws to a close, the temperatures drop down to a breathable level. When Sophie walks back, hair dripping once again, steamy water mounting from her shoulders, Claude nods and hands her a glass of wine. Sophie accepts and drifts away, impatient to return to London and the city's pace that will carry them from one hour on to the next.

Giulia does not seem to think that something has changed between the two friends either.

Claude

I don't use public transport. I cycle everywhere, within the remit of what is reachable. You would be surprised how far this territory extends: I do my grocery shopping; I deliver my baking goods; I go to visit the girls, Sophie in Mile End and Giulia in Battersea; I often cycle all the way to the sea. It's not so far if you are not aiming for the pretty beaches but only for the salty water. I have cycled back to the Rosary Boarding School, this place I entered and left only once, out of curiosity or perhaps what you might call nostalgia. I love my bike and the freedom it gives me, following my own path, away from strangers' habits. Exercising my freedom as one would strengthen a muscle. I also happen to be universal armpit-level height, which makes trains an acrid place to me. And I have one absurd fear: that if I do take public transport and fall asleep, someone – anyone – could draw a penis on my cheek. It happened once, when I got drunk away from Sophie for the first time. We were about to break off for Christmas and I had already decided that I wouldn't come back for the following term. I woke up, furry mouth and sticky eyes, on a stranger's sofa. I ran to the bathroom, feeling sick and sad. When I walked out, not having bothered to wash my face properly, I came face to face with Noah. He was tall, his eyes seemed to be pushed back deep in his face, giving him a coarse look. But he was tall and muscular. I'm still not sure if it was a coping mechanism for the embarrassment of having disgraceful body parts drawn on my face, or perhaps the hangover, or most likely I was still drunk. I lost my virginity that same night.

The weight of his tall body against mine, the hairy armpits against my chin, his sour sweat spitting onto my stomach, the smell of cold cigarettes coming from his dark hair and invading my throat, his eyes even more removed as they turned away from mine. He came. I did not move then, my eyes focused on the pixelated background behind him, while he removed himself, tied a knot at the end of the condom and threw it in the *Jurassic Park* dustbin on the other side of the room. I galloped back to my student accommodation, burning with a new desire. I wanted to look at myself in the mirror; I needed to inspect my swollen vagina. I wanted to picture what he had seen; to find again what he had stolen. It was early when I crossed Waterloo Bridge. All the buildings around me were radiant, the sunlight against them firing up powerful shades of gold, from silver to pink. It felt as if every single stream of light was directed towards my rotten bones, finding backlash in my greasy hair. I could already feel the pimple from the alcohol appearing on the left corner of my mouth. *Do I still have a penis tattoo?* This fear came to me as I jumped off my bike halfway across the bridge, falling on my knees, in a hurry to find my phone somewhere at the bottom of my bag. *Let it be charged, please.* 'Coffee? Xx' I texted Soph, even though I knew she would be fast asleep then. She sleeps until midday every Saturday; it gives her a healthy glow, she says. Since our times sharing a bunk bed, I've always been envious of Sophie's ability to sleep as if the world were a safe space, as if tomorrow was set to come and there was nothing to worry about in the dark.

I showered and lit up a Moka pot on one of my two hobs. These were old electric hobs waiting to set fire to our mouldy student accommodation. But we had a view of the Thames, just behind the Southbank Centre. Some of the buildings had slightly bigger rooms but the kitchen was common to everyone. Mine was a compact all-in-one room and I often dreamt I could transport it on small wheels and drive all the way to the South of France, picking up Maman on the way, bringing back our summertime car trips to the beach, the same CD by Sinéad O'Connor playing on the way there and back. A red swimsuit with shellfish motifs packed in my bag; salted butter spread on baguette for lunch, eager to taste the sea, afraid to swim; the small crystals that chapped our lips and dried our skin. We squinted our eyes fiercely to catch a sight of the French shores, but we never crossed the English Channel together. Maman has spent most of the years I have been alive locked down, with each reunion casting a spell over a future broken vow. She lives within four clean walls in an institution near Croydon, the same city that anchored her to England years ago. She first moved to London to learn English, the metropolis and language that promised her a secure job, she once confessed with watery eyes; then to the city's outskirt, Croydon, to afford rent – and raising me, though she never said that aloud. Our bond is cast on the backdrop of the memories we decide not to keep – Maman dreams of returning to France but my life is rooted in this island; this is a piece of knowledge I own and must live with. Her room is no bigger than mine was but she is not allowed to use the hob; she is fed by the nurse. *It's for the best*, since she once put her hand on her old hob. She crushed it against the red ceramic while I ate my saltless pasta, immobile from the top of my stool, too afraid to jump, frightened at the sight of physical pain. I was eight years old and growing rapidly.

While the coffee was brewing at a snail's pace, propagating a good smell and a sense of relief in my mind, I started whisking two eggs, a cup of plain flour and a cup of milk together. I whisked. I whisked. I whisked. I added a teaspoon of rum and set the bowl aside, with a tea towel for cover. I set up a small tray on my bed, with a jar of jam, half a lemon and white caster sugar. I sent a picture to Sophie, '*Waiting for you, sleeping beauty!*' It was ten to twelve and within the next ten minutes, I heard an enthusiastic knock on my door. Here she was, standing in front of me, with bad breath and messy hair, tangled in her duvet, the blanket following her like a cape. 'I am staaaarving,' she announced, and I closed the door behind her.

'Noah with the tiny eyes and long legs?' she asked, one dripping crêpe in her hand, her head resting on her left knee.

'It wasn't great. Not sure I'm that much into sex now I know what the whole fuss is about.'

'You've only tried once.'

'We did it five times,' I joked. A sting in my stomach strikes each time I picture my lying, winking face. How surreal this is to remember. A few minutes only, one man, how can it still be so sharp in my memory? Why can I not remember Maman's voice anymore but I can hear his groan so vividly? Wait. Silence. I can hear it now.

'I meant only one guy.'

'How many have you had?'

'I'm not the one that's not into sex.'

'Where is Dean these days?'

'He's busy with the rugby league. They went up a division this year.'

'Cool.'

I decided that sex was not something I was interested in. I mastered a loud enthusiastic voice and learnt enough sassy jokes to dismiss the conversation when someone brought it up. I am thankful that most talk of sex is preceded by quite a few drinks: whatever I said to pretend I had what is perceived as a healthy sex life was forgotten by dawn the next day. Then there was that blur of a summer, when Sophie graduated, when I worked long hours in a restaurant, carrying the plates I wished I had made. It was 2013. Sophie and Dean were running the show: he was a successful policy advisor for a *massive tech company* and Sophie was working for a *terrific couturier*, painting models' faces for the catwalk. Each time we went out, Dean came along, pushed by Sophie to bring his mates.

'For Claude; it's time we find her a boyfriend. Bring that one with the bright eyes, she likes that, Clo.' Silence. 'Yes, Stefan, that's the one.'

Every time it was the one. We grew apart as Sophie wanted to dine at restaurants to be seen, my yellow kitchen shrinking under the pressure of her ambitions. We fought as she lost more weight by the week, 'Do you even eat at those fancy restaurants you *a-d-o-r-e* so much?'

She stopped. We were outside a cocktail bar in Marylebone. The night had been long, Sophie ever so insistent on staying for one more, scanning the room, no longer looking me in the eye. I knew I had hurt her straight away: pale and fragile on the pavement. She crushed her cigarette under her left heel and went back inside. I missed her but I had to move on. I texted Stefan to see what he was up to. We had been texting on and off for a few weeks now; I think Dean was keen to find him a girlfriend too. He was nice, asking how my day went. We discussed our favourite movies and other vague hobbies through an uneventful thread of messages. I liked him. He gave me a sense of reassurance, you know? I was doing the right thing, showing interest in a man who was kind enough to ask questions, to welcome my attentiveness.

I'm out with the guys in Shoreditch. Nightcap?

Am West. Never mind, another time!

I'll take a cab. Share your location with me.

I sent my location and slid down against the wall. I didn't move for the next half hour or so. Stefan arrived and asked if I wanted to jump straight into his cab. It would be easier, he said. We mumbled a few ideas about where to go before we headed to his place. I had never been to a man's apartment before. The walls were so white and the rest so grey. He served us two glasses of white wine, a strange choice for this time of night, I thought. Why would he own this big television but not a liqueur? Why would he have such a modern kitchen but no ice in the freezer? We settled on the balcony and chatted aimlessly, elbows against the barrier, our eyes focused on the skyline ahead. I remember that I laughed heartily a few times. I enjoyed this man's perspective, one I had not really considered until now. It felt as if I was finally getting to know Dean a little, to have a glimpse into what Sophie's life was like. This domestic nest she puts so much energy into building, the tears I wiped away when men had not texted, said or done the exact thing she expected of them. Sophie shared the big things and the bad things; I wanted to experience the everyday. It was sweet and slow. He kissed me first and I questioned his choice of white wine once more. Bitterness. Dryness. The sourness, again. He gently smiled as he took my hand and walked me towards his bedroom. The sheets felt heavy in the empty room: one wardrobe and an alarm clock on the bedside table. He was tender throughout. I stayed still until the morning after. He woke up. I was so impatient; I wanted to discover the gaze he was going to use to look at me. Did I do well enough? He ran his finger down my stomach and I let him in. Straight afterwards he jumped out and into the bathroom. I exhaled. By the time he was out of the shower, I was dressed again. 'I really need to go. I have a shift this afternoon.'

'For the record, I was going to offer you breakfast,' he said, as I closed the door behind me. I called Sophie as I cycled back home after work and we made quick amends for the night before. I never told Sophie about Stefan, nor about what happened next.

★ ★ ★

I flicked through a few magazines. I tapped my heel against the bleached floor. I looked at my watch. Repeat. I heard my name from far away, 'Claude Thomas?' I turned towards the nurse. She smiled as I did. I followed her and we walked for what seemed like an eternity. I remember thinking that the clinic was certainly too small for the number of abortions that need to be executed every day. It was. I'm not alone. But how many can it be? How many are we? I have no idea. They don't share such numbers. I thought about my mother, trapped in another hospital. I wished I could speak to her, to ask her advice. Could she still smell the body fluids? The corridor stretched, the distance between the nurse and me lengthened: I was dreading the incision.

The nurse knocked on a door.

'Come on in,' someone shouted from inside. I shivered at the sound of the man's voice.

'Claude Thomas?'

I nodded. The nurse pulled a chair out for me. I sat, my legs tight, my two hands pushing firmly against my knees.

'I need to ask you a few questions before we start. Can you confirm your date of birth for me?'

'July 1991. 17 July 1991.'

Dry throat, I was looking for an escape when my eyes caught the notice about fire safety. A small but sharp laugh escaped, out of my control. The doctor stopped his interrogation.

'Sorry, the sign on the wall made me laugh. As if a fire is the biggest threat to people visiting the hospital.'

The nurse breathed in sharply.

'You realise this is a serious intervention I'm about to conduct?'

I nodded in silence.

The actual procedure lasted only a few minutes. I did not move, my focus settled on the bright neon lights on the ceiling, even when they turned into a blur. I remained still, my diaphragm set in stone, my cervix numb with anaesthesia. The doctor moved fast, knocking utensils back against the iron tray. The sharp clinking noises followed by a suction. *Can you hear it?* The feeling of air coming back through me as he slid out the bloody speculum. *Can you feel it?*

'You may experience bleeding and light pain for a few days, but you can resume your usual activities as soon as you feel well enough. If it worsens, call the clinic. You can take pain-killers in the meantime. Do you want some now? You're entitled to 1,000 milligrams of paracetamol on your way out,' he advised me as he removed both his gloves and mask. He stank of coffee. I refused the offer and walked out.

★ ★ ★

I can't remember the last time I felt such pain. I tried to lie still on my back; I lifted my legs up against the wall; I slowly walked in circles in the living room, all lights switched off; I tried not moving; I lifted up my bottom, a little bit only; I ran a hot bath, a lukewarm bath, a cold

bath. It was as if every single nerve in my body had transferred to my uterus, as if my brain had fallen down my
spine. I could not smell the mixture of piss, blood and
vomit from the hospital anymore. I turned off my phone
and took a deep breath. Two days passed. I didn't shower;
I was covered in sweat. It was the yellow shade that alerted
me. This colour I normally adore, the lemons in my jug
of water, the mustard I add to my vinaigrette, no longer
suited me. Would I ever taste mustard again? The yellow
of my kitchen walls looked ill. Two light purple circles
appeared underneath my eyes. The rest of my body was
yellow. Even my freckles seemed to have liquified into one
even tone: I did not recognise myself. I started texting
Sophie but felt discouraged as I glanced at the texts I had
received over the past few days, about boredom, about
Dean refusing to go to Spain for their summer holiday
because it will be too hot, the final question: Have you fallen
down your food processor????

It was the number of question marks that really got to me.
I gave in. I dialled 111. A few minutes later they connected me to the paramedics.

I woke up to find Giulia next to my bed, expressionless,
scrolling down her phone. I moved slightly; she jumped.

'Ciao, sweet pie. Turns out I'm your emergency contact.'
She grabbed my hands and held them tightly, 'I haven't
called her.'

I looked around the room. There were tubes going out

from my left arm into a monitor – my skin was yoghurt-pale. I almost missed the yellow. I could not smell it anymore, the hospital. I wished I could, then. *Will I ever be able to taste again?* I worried.

Giulia continued, 'You lost consciousness on the way here, exhausted from fighting this mighty infection. Would you like me to read what's in the tubes? It's all listed on here.'

Giulia was pointing out a little notepad, clipped at the end of the bed. I was relieved Giulia was my emergency contact. I was grateful for her calm approach and ability to embrace my clinical thinking. I nodded.

'So. Madonna. This is gonna be a tough one, bear with me, darling. Clindamycin 900 milligrams IV every eight hours; Gentamicin 5 milligrams per kilo IV once a day; Ampicillin 2 grammes IV every four hours.' Giulia was enunciating the words carefully and I slowly teared up in the background, washing the foreign fluids out of my body. Giulia looked up then: 'Do you want to play with the bed?'

She threw the remote at me.

I didn't move.

'Half of the time I regret it,' I said.

I knew straight away that I will always remember Giulia's look, she who is normally so abrupt and not one for dissecting an emotion. Giulia sat back gently and nodded at me as a sad smile wrinkled in the corner of her mouth. She looked as if she knew this moment would come and she had prepared. She was not going to steal my words, she quietly waited instead. I might have misread her but she looked proud.

'Sleeping with men. Half of the time I regret it.'

She considered me carefully, the absurdity of the situation perhaps. She simply replied, 'So why do you do it?'

'Because half of the time I don't,' she let me continue. 'It's nice to feel like I belong. You know, it's worth it.' I closed my eyes, tired suddenly, hit by the wave of choices we repeatedly make. Wholemeal or rye bread; yes or no to the Brexit referendum; change for the Victoria Line at King's Cross or Euston; visit Maman this week or not.

As if she'd read my mind, Giulia plunged in. 'You should call Sophie when you get out of here. I know she will want to hear from you.'

Giulia stayed until the very last minute of visiting hours. We spent the last hour plotting how she could sneak back in at night, tearing up from laughter. Giulia is a tonic, her body jumping through life at a fast pace. She never stops and I don't know where she is most of the time, but she is always running back to me when I need her. She left and I took my phone out. I ignored all the notifications and typed quickly: Soph! Been taken away by an awful flu. Sorry I did not text before, been sleeping all this time. Is there still a world out there??? Should be back in the next 48 hours or so. Xx

I turned off the light but not my thoughts.

Autumn

1

The air is sour. The warmest summer the planet has ever known is reaching its peak and there is an ambient dread in the air, the leaves already turning brown, burnt by the sun. The pavement smells of grilled dust.

'Is it too early for an ice-cold gin and tonic?' asks Sophie as Giulia embraces her.

They are walking towards Victoria Park. The mud that envelops the potatoes stored in front of the convenience shops has never smelt so strong. It is dry these days. They are tempted to stop for dates, sweet and filling, sticky little pleasures. But the bottle of Georgian white wine is more attractive. If they were believers, they might have called this a sign but instead they continue to chat as they follow the lead from the ice cream van. The familiar music beckons them but they do not need to see the white and red vehicle to know where it will park. They have bought many 99 Flakes from this van over the years, Giulia sealing their transaction with the word *outrageous* (in reference to the pricing of ice creams) every single time they do. Her remark has become a regular sound in Sophie's ears, similar to the music of a cash register closing in the intro of the Pink Floyd song, or like one of the colourful machines made of plastic they owned when they were small girls playing shopkeepers, when prices were either *expensive as gold* or £1, when they attached excitement to a price tag in quest of ownership and little of the emotional drain that money now triggers. Today they feel embarrassed about their cashier games as they grow anxious that they might never be able to afford the adult life they had forecast for themselves. Sophie brushes Giulia's remark away with a complicit smile as she reaches for the dripping cone. They keep walking, followed by the noise of Sophie's sandals clapping against her heels. They stop by the small chemist to buy sunscreen, suddenly struck by how hot the day is. They sit on the grass so they can finish their ice creams.

Giulia smiles at Sophie.

'Come on, then.'

'Sophie, do you know why we call a 99 Flake a 99 Flake?'

Sophie rolls her eyes, even though she loves this story.

'Once upon a time in the 1920s, the Italians were up in the County of Durham, making some soft ice creams for their cousins the Brits. It wasn't so hot then but you know, you guys love a sweet thingy.' She pushes her arms towards the sky and Sophie laughs at how radiant she looks. Giulia is vocal about the fact that she does not miss Italy and that she cannot see herself moving back, but the smile on her face each time she mentions her mother country tells another story. She continues, 'So they decided to add extra flavour to their softies, with a Cadbury Flake inserted inside.' With an expression of disgust on her face, she takes a break to lick her melting lemon sorbet. 'Turns out it worked out quite well for them, so the new combination was in need of a name. You Brits always love a little royal feel to things, so the Italians thought back to their own kings. At the time, the monarchy in Italy had a guard made up of ninety-nine men so anything really special was known as novantanove. And that ice cream is so royal that we called it the 99 Flake.'

Sophie bursts out into loud laughter, as she has done after each telling of this story over the years.

Claude would have laughed too.

Giulia is animated now, riding high on Sophie's giggles and the memory of her own childhood. 'My opinion is that those smart-ass Italian workers took you for the fools you are.'

'The ninety-nine guards are what really gets to me,' adds Sophie. 'Like the ultimate sign of sophistication is not to need a hundred guards but only ninety-nine.'

On any given summery day, they would have continued this staged dialogue for long enough to outlast their ice creams, drifting on to a debate about the monarchy. Claude would have screamed 'be more Versailles, behead them!' And Giulia would have met her chanting friend with sparkling eyes and an explosive smile. Pain, similar to a needle that extracts blood from a vein, would have struck Sophie. Then Claude and Giulia would have started performing some of the soundtrack from the Sofia Coppola movie about Marie Antoinette, the one they have watched more times than they have fingers to lick the drizzling sugar from their ice creams. Sophie would have rolled her eyes before adding, 'They bring in so much money with all the tourism. The Germans love them!' They would have paused then, and Sophie would have brought them back together, summarising: 'But . . . they also cost a lot more money!' They would have laughed; they really would have laughed on such a hot day in their favourite London park together. But on the edge of autumn 2019, everything feels different. Claude and Sophie exchanged brief text messages after they returned from their Lisbon escape – weather memes, satirical tweets, alarming news articles – yet nothing pushed them to meet, and so they stopped. Sophie said she needed a break to look after herself and Claude retreated. It is after all the end of the hottest of all summers on earth: the sugar from the ice cream leaves their tongues numb.

Giulia did not appear as surprised as Sophie had feared she would when she first envisaged their conversation, before telling her about the episode in the Lisbon bathroom, about the shared dream of a house in Provence, only a few days after they landed back in London. She allows herself to wonder, is that because everyone is in some sort of love with their best friend? But not everyone has slept with their best friend. Or have they, and she simply doesn't know about it? Sophie recalls the tingling sensation in her forearms as she listened to people's monologues about searching for a 'best friend' in a partner, in life, onscreen, in books. She thinks carefully and longingly about what they meant, about this constant search for the 'best' of people and the 'best' in one person; a search for someone else to be a better person than you are. Is it the physical act that makes her and Claude a different pair from the trio they have with Giulia? Is the second when they both gasped for air as they lay back the moment it was redefined? She had never felt her body lifted as delicately – empathically – as when she was naked alongside Claude. The assurance with which their hands had moved; it was more than being penetrated – it was more like being considered; the feeling of being truthful with the other. It is not the act of having sex with Claude that changed everything, it is the fact that there is no going back from what her body has sensed. To engage sexually with Claude is a political act and Sophie does not want to bring politics back to bed with her; fever dreams looming, cold sweat pearling down her back.

Giulia elbows Sophie, 'What's up?'

'It hurts. My forearms, they hurt.'

Giulia nods in concerned silence before Sophie goes on: 'It started a few weeks ago. Like it really does hurt. It's so odd, you know. For something as basic as a forearm to hurt so much. It's like it's been in your life from day one and you never really gave it much attention because it's just there. For you to do anything, you need that forearm to operate. It's always there, in between you and anything you're trying to reach. And then it starts hurting and you understand you have always underestimated that forearm of yours.' There are quiet tears running down Sophie's cheeks. She can hear little voices in her head – buzzing little memories that are abruptly cut short by the teacher who once found her and the girls playing under the oak tree back in school, shouting unintelligibly, slapping her apron against her thigh as she walked towards their sitting circle. The violence with which she picked up the milk bottle, the disgust on her face as she too felt the stickiness; small white traces of lactose against her palm.

Do you think proper girls play this game?

'We're in love. I'm in love with Claude.'

'Aren't we all?' Giulia slowly swallows. 'The three of us, haven't we always been in love?'

Sophie turns back to look at her friend and nods. 'I mean, the way you love Teddy. The way you love Ted, that's how we love one another, Claude and I.'

Giulia hurts. She loves the way she loves Teddy but she also wishes she could be part of this love Claude and Sophie share. Is she letting them down by not loving them this way?

'Don't let me make this about myself. Have you told Claude any of this?'

'That my forearms hurt?'

'No. That you love her, romantically.' Giulia doesn't hide her annoyance, spitting out the latter word slowly. 'If you have always loved one another, if you are so sure of it, what are you waiting for?'

'I can't love Claude the way she wants me to. It's between us this love we have.' Sophie pauses, her lips continue to move nervously but quietly. She closes her eyes before picking up the pace again: 'I can't allow our intimacy to become others' business, not when it's always been there for the two of us.'

'I don't understand, Soph. I really don't. You're the one making this about the rest of the world. I see two brilliant women who love one another, had bloody good sex and want to have more. I say brava!' Giulia's attempt to lighten the mood runs dry, however much she rolls her 'r's. She finds it hard to witness them sharing these feelings she cannot be a part of, harder since it will get in the way of the three of them spending time together.

'Claude is not the only woman in my life, Giulia. You know that. You know my mother is always there too.'

Giulia is left with the picture of thin, long-faced, ashy-white-bob-topped Allegra. 'She has developed a cough and got thinner,' Sophie adds, as if she had seen her as well.

They are both quiet, lost in their thoughts. But there is nothing to say. The air has become stiffer between the two friends. They stay silent for a while longer. Sophie is holding her left wrist with her right hand. There are no diamonds left on her fingers, something she is reminded of every day as she brushes her teeth, as she washes the dishes, as she picks up her phone. It is *that* she is grieving, not the jewellery but the image of it; the cracked trophy. It was so much easier to love Dean: they both lived their lives in parallel, finding each other again at home at the end of the day. There was nothing special about Dean and Sophie being together and she loved that. Anyone discovering a photo of the two of them in fifty years' time would say *what a beautiful pair. I bet he loved her dearly.* Who would throw that away? Aren't we all told that in the end the most beautiful of love stories are the undramatic ones? That you know you are in love when there is no fight for it, when you surrender to the other person and it feels like a satisfying ballad. Allegra had warned her, *You won't find a better fit than Dean, Sophie. Poor Dean, all the investment he put into this relationship. You silly, spoilt girl.* Does she remember her mother's words correctly? She knows time edits conversations from the past. Isn't Claude the love of her life? It – she – had always been there. This love, an organic love. But how can love transcend when she cannot recall ever having seen a happy, flawless queer love depicted on the thousands of screens she has watched, in the hundreds of lines she has read?

Giulia knows better than to express her opinion about Allegra. She respects the hierarchy as she reaches out to Sophie's shoulders instead, shaking her gently. There is nothing else to add, not today at least, so they pick up their conversation and broaden it. The Labour Party conference just happened last week, the Conservative one is due the following week. Uber's right to trade is expiring in London and Sophie fears the prospect of getting back on the bus after a long night at work. She is doing brilliantly: *a make-up artist who is breaking common ground*, some online fashion blogs have recently written about her and the growing business she is shaping up, born from her hardworking fingers and enhanced via Allegra's network. Giulia reminds Sophie that the Conservative Party is more dangerous than a double-decker bus with its brakes cut. 'Both have cameras everywhere, though,' she concludes with a reassuring, tender smile. They laugh in relief and then they are quiet again. They need breaks throughout, to fight against the small emotions that threaten to burst out of their mouths. They wish they could scream. Neither of them wants to come across as angry – it would not be helpful, they respectfully think in silence. The afternoon continues until they part ways, Sophie returning to Allegra's house where she now lives.

When she broke off the engagement with Dean, her moving back in with Allegra was introduced as a self-evident solution. 'The Mile End apartment reminds me too much of him.' She sold the flat she had always hated. It was a Thursday, early in September, when she travelled back to East London to tidy and clean up Dean's leftovers, before the men and a van she hired were due to arrive and remove any clues of the failed-to-be-marriage. She received a worrisome number of messages that day – from colleagues and friends she rarely sees; from Allegra and her father – sending their love and support on this *difficult day*. Giulia shared a playlist, featuring Fleetwood Mac, David Bowie and the Supremes – the only bit of attention Sophie really appreciated. There was no feeling of sadness left in Sophie that day, only excitement. She hated the place. How many times did she need to say it so the people who live alongside her would see it too? She turned on the old stereo she had bought during her last year of university; it had a thin lead on the left-hand side to plug in your phone and was not as unreliable as Dean's deluxe Bluetooth appliance. Sound on; headband tying her hair back. She set herself in motion, dancing, sweating, screaming around the flat. The anger. How could she feel so strongly about four walls? She wished she had an axe. She could have torn the place apart if all sense of self control had left her. She swears she could have. She had put so much work into making this apartment lovely for them: colourful plants and bookshelves, a sustainable pantry for the rainy days, the photos up on the walls in the corridor, featuring both sides of the family equally, there was always toothpaste in the bathroom. It was a perfectly fine flat. There was even a second bedroom. And a balcony. She turned the music up louder and continued to dance through the flat, packing boxes with objects among a cloud of dust, leaving the items that reminded her of Dean behind.

She started to itch, a sudden sense of warmth running up from her toes. The windows were all wide open. She drank a glass of water. It did not pass. It was burning down her body; it smelt sweet. Not long afterwards, her hands ran down her stomach. She was not sure if she felt more embarrassed or ridiculous at first. But the excitement came fast enough. All these hours she has spent in the bathroom, scrubbing, waxing, hydrating. How did her fingers never slip down to her clitoris before? She continued, standing in the middle of her spotless kitchen, one hand pushing against the fridge, the other navigating her vagina, granting it a renewed right to exist, to feel. It did feel good. She conquered it: her body. She could feel it coming in waves – liberation – as all fear left her, as she controlled the pace, as she savoured breaks from her moving fingers, sensing the heat running up her body. Thrilling. She felt strong, standing on her two legs, oblivious to the noise her fluids made, her left hand venturing away from the fridge and towards her breast. *I'm doing this,* she said out loud. *I'm fucking myself.* In the kitchen, among the polished light grey cupboards, where she was supposed to cook Sunday roast for her perfect family, so they said. She pushed strongly against the shiny white floor. It was not long until she really understood. She had come home, embraced by her body and its renewed desires. The years of grooming, of hunger, the scars from the ingrown hairs she pushed into her skin over time, polished nails. Who were those for? She pulled her trousers back up, her mouth feeling syrupy. She packed boxes for another hour or so.

Sophie slammed the door behind her.

2

When Giulia jumps onto the Northern Line after work, it had already been Friday in her mind for the last forty-eight hours. She is joining Teddy for a drink at the pub, and then they might walk to the cinema. What she loves about the late shift at work is the seat on the Tube. She settles in the first carriage, letting her body lean heavily on the Plexiglas, slumping after a week of watching her posture on the office chairs. The smell alerts her first, a sweetness slowly growing in her nostrils. She slides her tongue against her teeth. When the fast-paced, jingling noise begins, she forcibly opens her eyes. She notices two women next to her, and finds herself envious of their freedom. She would never dare to confess such a thought to Claude, or even Sophie – she doesn't want anyone to call her a *bad feminist*, accusing her of feeding the beauty myth. Look at them, though: bags wide open, powder flying around, sticky cherry gloss on the tip of their fingers, cans of pink gin and tonic open in their hands. They share a pair of headphones between the two of them, sometimes nodding at a faster pace, their hair staying still. The choreography of their fingers moving, drawing straight lines, complacent eyes on their compacts. She envies their lightness of being, celebrating their friendship. They run out at Camden Town.

Giulia digs out her phone and scans her face in the mirror of her screen. She unties her bun, letting her curls fall down her shoulders. She adds red lipstick. *Lady danger* she mutters to herself, triggering a faint smile. She has been dating Teddy for almost five months now. For years she swiped through apps, getting her heart broken by a man she only met twice, building elaborate scenarios of what might have happened to the men who never replied, spending a fortune in rounds of drinks to hear about the last movie the man in question did not watch. All these dates she never mentioned to anyone, ashamed and tired at the simple thought of telling the story, her secretive nights. She is confident she can advise anyone about a career in finance now. The hours she has spent flattering egos that are not hers. Teddy is a nice guy and she likes that about him. He rarely reads between the lines and does not anticipate many of her needs aside from hunger, but then she is always hungry. He is a perfectly nice guy. He picks up the phone when she calls and will listen to all the details she likes to add to the stories from home – if Giulia is going to tell you about how her cousin is, you first need to know how the neighbour is, which leads on to what happened at the local bar yesterday. There is a butterfly effect to anything in Giulia's life, or so she believes.

Who will be my bridesmaids? Giulia surprised herself by thinking when they came back from Lisbon. That is another thought she won't share with her friends, Sophie recovering from her broken engagement, Claude despairing at the traditional spin of her friends' dreams. It hurts. It really does hurt when your dreams are crushed. Even more so when your best friends are the ones who squeeze each picture you built for your future photo albums, who strain your fantasies until landscapes fade and colours dry. Giulia loves her friends and she loves men and she really wants a first dance. It will make her Nonna so happy. And Marija. Once they have met Teddy. She hasn't told them yet, although they both find it suspicious that Giulia does not always take their calls anymore. She will tell them next time she goes back to Italy because that is a conversation to be had at their kitchen table. She wants Nonna to hold her hands – *bellissima, la mia bella Giulia*. She is already smiling at the thought of her mother rushing around the house to show her the photos from her wedding with Paolo again. She wants to hear the story being retold even though she already knows this tale by heart. Giulia is the one who handed Marija and Paolo the rings to celebrate this new union and her mother's second chance. That is a story to be shared, one Marija cherishes and wants her daughter to hold on to as part of their family's narrative, one moment that makes a daughter look up to her mother. Giulia would never dare to ask about the man who gave her her genetic identity, about the blood that beats through her heart. He does not make her mother look good, Marija's face closing at each mention. She misses them every day, especially when Claude and Sophie fail to be her family. What she loves about their trio is how they always seem to find space for one another, regardless of their frustrations, other commitments and the state of the world. Like a family. She loves the love between her two friends. She seeks time with them separately: the impulsive Sophie, who led them to dance floors across London, day trips and other journeys through countries and the years; the attentive Claude, and her refusal to go to sleep until she has found a solution to your problem, her invitation to be part of her kitchen. But she loves them the most when they are together. They remind her of Paolo and Marija. The constant electricity in the air caused by the chemistry of two fundamentally different brains, sealed by the mellowness of their hopeless romantic hearts. She misses her families. She would never tell them that.

When she finally reaches the pub, Teddy is waiting for her with two pints. She wishes he had waited because she was in the mood for red wine. He smiles as soon as she opens the door and she drops the thought of arguing over something as short-sighted as a pint of beer. They can be a family together.

3

Claude styles her hair shorter now. She always wears colourful hoop earrings and never wears anything else on her feet other than her two-tone derby shoes. *She is just very cool*, Sophie thought when Claude entered the pub. She is finding the silence between them difficult but it would be more challenging to break it. It feels discouraging to realise how you can grow to love someone even more when you do not see them.

There are about twenty people in the room – some familiar, some unknown faces – to celebrate Nick turning thirty years old. This milestone their generation has been working towards, heads down, since they hit their mid-twenties. The weather has been radiant all week but today the clouds are pouring down: Nick's long hair, Claude's short hair, the furry dog, they all smell of old coins, soaking wet. They drink more to keep warm, there are balloons tied to one of the chairs, loud laughter echoing from the bare walls and high ceilings, implying that they will only get louder as the day continues to fade. They all dread Nick's speech because they know he will give one. He won't do it now because he wants them to stay as long as possible, and nobody wants to leave before the starring moment of the night. None of them wants to be the one receiving the text tomorrow, which will appear on their screens in a snapshot, *omg you missed the most hilarious moment when* . . . The hangover would feel even more dreadful if it did not grant them the right to be quoted in future memories.

'Thank you all for coming to this lifetime event, the one of an all right guy turning thirty. I always thought by now I would be able to compare myself a little more to my parents but that day has not come.' Break for laughter. 'I still don't have the job I wanted to have, which is retirement, so I look forward to the next thirty-four years.' They all raise a glass. 'I might not be so young anymore, but the night is.' Claude and Sophie look at one another and roll their eyes. 'Please be wild. I intend to be. There will be more drinks involved and Giulia ordered food.' The university friends laugh, their eyes moving away from Nick, towards Giulia, whose stare remains still but with a glint. Nick continues but as he goes further into his speech, catching up with his present life, there is little space left for the older friends. The man he has become or the one he wants them to picture – self-confident; self-accomplished; self-sufficient – is not the Nick from their university days. 'So everyone, to me and my glorious life – may it be long!' Everyone raises their glass before breaking into their separate social bubbles.

Nick's speech, if one can call a ramble in front of a crowd a speech, has brought a taste of rust into Sophie's mouth.

The Yellow Kitchen

This story of time passing; the length of a life. It was only yesterday that cold days and burning nightmares ended with the warmth of Claude's body. *I always hated that school. My home in Hampstead was so bright, the stainless white walls and the cedar wooden floor, perfectly waxed. The Rosary was a row of long corridors, floors and walls covered in this old, creaking wood, this very dark oak. Lightless. Hopeless. The occasional crucifix hanging on top of a doorframe, overlooking us girls for no other reason than the fact that everyone was too afraid to remove them. I saw those crucifixes coming to life at night, feverish and feeling my body drowning in the squeaky bed. Clo, are you awake? I whispered, pressing my right hand through the barrier of her bed. Claude squeezed it. Nobody ever caught us, because I was the most discreet when it came to keeping my Clo close. The feeling of safety as our bodies aligned, my heart still pounding strong but for the right reasons this time. Our first kiss.* The music has suddenly grown louder. Sophie goes to the bar to order another drink, where she meets Hana and Candice in the queue. They go for a bottle of white wine and settle together, standing against the end of the counter. The view of the room from there is the best.

'You know what's the worst about dating?' asks Hana, who has recently broken up with Elliott; Giulia texted Sophie as soon as the news broke a few weeks ago.

'The worst?'

'That's a tough one,' says Sophie, not really paying attention, her eyes venturing around the room.

Hana continues: 'It's all these movies I wish I had watched on my own or with a mate rather than with a random guy. So many good movies I wasted on dates.' She drinks. There is a respectful silence, allowing them to grieve the hobbies they donated to their dates.

'And all the bars that don't feel new anymore.'

'All the bars you cannot go to anymore because they feel haunted.' They chuckle.

'Sex. All the sex I could have had on my own.' The silence is longer, heavier, this time. This is uncharacteristic of Sophie, she knows; she is the one who ends the unpleasant awkwardness with a sharp laugh. 'What? Have you not had bad sex?'

'Are you dating much already?'

'Not so much. I've been scrolling though the apps, nothing special.'

'Which app?' replies Candice, with the excitement only someone who already is in a partnership can feel for dating apps. Hana and Sophie eye one another, linked by the frustration of having to keep your bored friends entertained with your dating life. They give in anyway; the music isn't so great and Sophie doesn't want to feel Claude's body anywhere near hers. Not here. She grabs her phone and they swipe right and left for a few minutes. Are Sunday roasts really a thing, then? Why is everyone proudly advertising how many countries they have lived in when they try to brand themselves as a safe guy to date? What is it about David Attenborough that makes him so lovable to all? And the dogs – they really are the ones the dating apps are made for.

Claude, Giulia and a woman they just met in the bathroom are dancing. It is a blissful night, sliding into October.

4

Sophie wakes up around three o'clock in the morning. Her pyjamas feel clammy against her skin. She is shivering. She looks at her phone and wonders if Claude, Giulia and the other woman are still dancing. She is certain they are. She falls back onto her bed. She rolls from one side to the other. Fast, still sweating, still shivering. She goes down the stairs, towards the kitchen, and pours herself a glass of cold water. The liquid slowly slides down her throat. She remembers her doctor's advice from her first attack – *pour a glass of ice-cold water, swallow slowly, if the pain down your thorax* (at which point he had pressed his thumb against the top of her ribs, between her breasts, for longer than felt needed) *stops or at least diminishes, then you know you are not having a heart attack, only a panic attack*. A panic attack, that's all. Only a panic attack.

The second panic attack she remembers is the first one she had with Claude there. It was a stormy morning and they were unaware of the rain they had called upon themselves, them and the girls sitting in a circle underneath the oak tree. *Do you think proper girls play this game?* is what their teacher had asked them. They should have known better.

Sophie ran through the long corridors and sat upright on the ice-cold tile flooring in the bathroom. Claude had followed her, *Soph? Are you in there?* She had cautiously asked before pushing the door open. They sat together, Sophie panting fast, Claude's thoughts running even faster to fix her friend. She pushed herself against Sophie – not holding her but tenderly scooping her body against hers – announcing that they were going to count until ten together, except they were going to do so in French, because it would take longer.

Claude started to count, her lips moving with caution: 'Un, deux, trois, quatre, cinq, six, sept, huit, neuf, dix.' Then she turned her face towards her friend, 'Do you see it now? The beige house in Provence, with the lavender for a fence?'

Sophie shook her head, still panting.

Claude continued: 'Onze, douze, treize, quatorze, quinze, seize, dix-sept, dix-huit, dix-neuf, vingt.' Twenty is when Sophie grabbed Claude's hand, as she started to picture their future house too. They both stood.

Sophie begins to count slowly, back in London, pouring herself another glass of water between each new decimal. Blood. Spiders. Thunder. Elevators. Knees. Swallowing. Everything she is afraid of is rushing back to her mind now. She continues to count until she remembers the house in

Provence. Claude has taught her the numbers up to one hundred since that first time together.

Sophie misses Claude.

* * *

Claude passes her front door soon after midnight, her shoes feel tighter, making each step a struggle, her tired muscles and fizzy brain guiding her through to the yellow kitchen. She brings water to the boil, a mechanical step that turns the liquid as salty as the sea she wishes to soak her body in. *We used to crawl through the corridors at night, giggles caught in the spiderwebs of our elbows and pyjamas, all the way to the kitchen. We fooled Mrs Swann most of the time, although we collected a few hours of detention along the way.* Claude stands in front of her cupboards, a pack of spaghetti in one hand, her eyes browsing for comfort, something warm and nutritious. She is shivering, the gin and tonic bringing her blood sugar to a low. A can of chopped tomatoes, a pinch of salt, half a teaspoon of brown sugar and a few black olives simmer next. *Mrs James headed the canteen at the time, her shouting voice and burgundy cheeks preceded her reputation. She knew about our midnight adventures. Her appetite and kindness sealed our secret agreement as she left sample spices for us to try behind the fridge. She wrote a few facts about each spice – turmeric, paprika or even spirulina – on small Post-it notes for us to find.* Claude adds paprika to the thickening tomato sauce and returns to the shelves where she finds a tin of sardines. The fish squishes under the weight of her fork, the small bones reduced to a mash, she swallows one spoonful and incorporates the rest into the tomatoey mixture. The heat is reduced to a minimum. More salt in the shape of capers this time. *I tasted each spice Mrs James had hidden for us to find meticulously, both individually and combined. I took notes as I did. Sophie made eyeshadows with their powder; the tips of her fingers ran under a trickle of cold water first so the colours would stick to our skin. 'Pretty please, pretty Clo, will you be my doll?' We sat cross-legged on the kitchen floor, among the smell of dried milk, my eyes closed under Sophie's long hands, making one another shine.* Claude runs a cold stream of water from the tap before she drains the pasta. She has reserved a small amount of cooking water, which she now adds to the mixture as she combines spaghetti and tomato sauce together. The deep and heavy sky outside strengthens the lighting in the kitchen with ferocity.

Claude stands still before her hob, the same fork she used to cook now fishing for a first taste of pasta. *We giggled through the nights then, all the way until we graduated. Sophie was to launch a famous make-up brand and I was going to open a seasonal bakery. Together, in London. Until the year of 2010: a volcano erupted in Iceland and turned the air thicker than ever. Sophie enrolled at the London College of Fashion and I went on to study English Literature, guided by a scholarship, an opportunity that was described as one that cannot be refused. There was an overall sense of pressure to consume life fast, while it lasted.* She smiles but her eyes are watery, gulping down another mouthful of pasta. Maman. The smell of tea. Wolves. Eggshells. Selfish acts. Thoughts rush on but Claude continues to knit pasta through the tines of her fork, the looping spaghetti, the anchoring salty tomato sauce. Claude returns to the door, her sticky hands digging for her phone that is buried somewhere in one of her coat pockets. She replies to Giulia so her friend knows she has also arrived home safely. Then, she opens her chat with Sophie but she locks her phone away before she can message her. Claude returns to the hob and covers the pan, the leftover pasta sitting at the bottom, the tinned sardines will reemerge in small puddles of oil overnight. There is no good in ignoring Sophie. Claude switches the lights off and heads to bed just before the hour hand reaches one o'clock in the morning.

Claude misses Sophie.

5

Saturday morning at the local market: Claude strolls down the crowded street, stopping to speak with the various shop owners she has got to know over the years. They call themselves the family of local producers since they formed a union years back, inheriting stall spots from one generation to another, a thread of continuity that brings Claude confidence about the place where she has anchored her life. Claude goes to the market every week, a small pinch in her stomach and her copy of the weekend edition of *Libération* newspaper in her bag. She remembers how lovingly her mother spoke about the markets, though she never witnessed her marching through one. The Sunday markets made of clustered white tents, featuring everything from shoes and soap to jewellery and eggs in the car parks of French towns, are the ones her mother wanted to attend.

Claude has just passed Robin the fishmonger when she notices a new vintage clothes tent. She is surprised it sits so closely to the fish; the fabrics will most certainly absorb the pungent smell. She walks in and finds herself trying on a few jacquard suit jackets, all of which are under £20, a pleasing sight to Claude who is convinced she does not need a suit jacket.

'It would look lovely with a pair of black jeans and a simple white tee-shirt,' says the shop assistant. She has wild, long hair and is wearing a green maxi dress. She adds that she also has great coats, all selling for less than a third of their original value, and she has heard London will be hit by one of its coldest winters, she is sure of this forecast, oh yes, after the summer they've had, it can only continue to go wrong. It is scary. Doesn't she think so? She can distinctly remember the four seasons of her childhood but now it feels as if the world has fallen into this binary mode, with two seasons for reference only. Claude lets out a sharp laugh at the word *binary*. The woman finds the coats online mainly, from private sellers, then she fixes them in her attic at home and gets them dry-cleaned. They have all been checked for bedbugs, not to worry. Can Claude smell the lovely lavender spray she uses? Claude hates the smell of dried lavender, a paltry replacement for the one of lavender bushes, sweet and wild, when experienced in their natural habitat.

Enter another woman. She has thin, grey hair and is walking with the help of a crutch. She announces herself with a bright and loud salutation. The shop owner lets her know that she has coats and Claude rolls her eyes towards the sky at the thought of winter being introduced again, at the prospect of having to take part in pre-empting what the future might bring with two strangers. Turns out the old lady could really use a coat. It is wet in the morning when she walks her Cavalier King Charles dog. She needs something to protect her from the humidity, especially since her lungs are not as strong anymore. Bruno needs long walks, which is good as it forces her to move. Claude wonders who calls their dog *Bruno* — isn't that a human name? *He was mastered by the sheer surging of life, the tidal wave of being, the perfect joy of each separate muscle, joint, and sinew in that it was everything that was not death, that it was aglow and rampant, expressing itself in movement, flying exultantly under the stars and over the face of dead matter that did not move.* She remembers, echoes from her childhood bathtub, her mother's dream of a dog, Buck howling in her ears. Her muscles ache. Her hands slide against her waist, she looks at the projection of herself in the mirror. Claude is absent. *What name would Maman have given to our family dog if we had one? Would we have walked the dog together? Would we have sat for dinner together, if we were obliged to feed a dog routinely every day?*

'Could you help me?' the old woman interrupts. She is handing her crutch to Claude, a long black coat in her other hand.

Claude nods and the woman tries on the piece of clothing. 'What do you think?'

'It suits you.'

The woman starts again with her account of walking her dog Bruno every morning, as if Claude wasn't listening the first time. Claude waits patiently.

'It seems like it suits your needs, then,' she adds politely.

'I haven't bought something like this in a long time.'

'Clothes?'

'Something for myself that was not only for consumption, you know, food, petrol, a drink. But that seems all right. I do need a waterproof coat.'

Claude continues to nod, pinching her lips tight together, as she craves to know if the old lady has bought one of those tiny coats made for dogs for her Bruno.

'Would you buy it?'

'Oh,' Claude starts mumbling, fidgety at the thought of this question, a breach of her intimacy. 'I'm not sure, but I do not know if I need a coat either.'

'If you were me, would you?'

Claude's eyes are itchy; they feel as if they've doubled in size. The dazzling punch in the stomach caused by this older woman's expectation of Claude to know what will suit her. Surely the woman knows best what suits her needs. How could *she* know and why is she expected to know? She is feeling dizzy suddenly, taken aback by the thought of how many selfies she has sent to Sophie and Giulia from the various fitting rooms she has entered, hopeful to discover a new piece of clothing that will fit her curves, incapable of making the decision on her own, not until someone else would say it: *You look pretty, Claude.* This is what happens when you only live with a dog: they cannot pick up the phone when you need them. *The Call of the Wild. Bloody Buck.* It is them who need you. *Was it because I didn't know what might suit your needs that you left, Maman?* Sophie would have known what to reply to the old woman – where is the shop assistant? Surely this is her decision to make.

'If what you are looking for is a coat to protect you from the rain, then it seems appropriate.'

The old woman smiles as she looks down at herself again in the mirror resting on the floor. Claude grabs it to level it up, so she can also see the top of her body.

'Thank you, dear. It is a little loose on the shoulders.'

'But you might want to put an extra layer underneath in a few weeks,' Claude adds, a frail smile emerging.

'You're right. OK, I'll buy it.'

Claude leaves the vintage shop but the jacquard jackets stay behind, today is a Saturday to look ahead. Onwards, on to the fruit and vegetables stall, she is smiling.

6

Claude is putting her groceries away when Giulia rings the bell. She is not expecting anyone – she never is – and for a split second, she feels ashamed that her friends always assume she will be home, available to open the door for them, not needing to announce themselves before they travel to her flat. On the other side of the door, she can hear her friend panting. She feels proud now that Giulia chose to run all the way to her flat to visit her. Giulia walks directly to the tap, pouring herself a large glass of water. She drinks. Pours more water into her glass. Drinks some more, while Claude opens the window.

Claude waits, arms crossed.

'Twenty kilometres,' Giulia announces as she takes off her smartwatch and walks towards the balcony. 'It's so nice out there, you wouldn't think November is around the corner. I don't want it to be November. Should we move to Rome? You'll bake cakes and I will start my own marketing agency for cooks across Italy. All those Europeans moving to Italy to start their own restaurants, they need rebranding.' She is talking fast. These are the innocent dreams Claude and Giulia thrive on when they get together. Sophie struggles to see Italy as a country other than a warm holiday destination, they acknowledge with a shared spark in their pupils.

'How was your first week?' asks Claude, speaking slowly, hoping the rhythm of her words will help her friend to loosen up. Giulia started a new job on Monday, again, in the constant midst of building a career, with no clearer words than the broad 'marketing' and 'account manager' titles to define her path. She is avoiding eye contact so Claude invites Giulia to come back to the yellow kitchen. 'I found some beautiful apples at the market. Let's make a crumble.'

Claude starts opening the cupboards, blood awakening through her short legs again, working butter with her hands and measuring flour. Giulia is leaning against the fridge and the smell of coffee is building up across the kitchen. She is feeling confident, her new job is going fine, *enjoying it so far*, slowly getting to grips with what needs to be done. She hasn't felt so welcomed by her colleagues, though. They don't seem to drink coffee. Not even tea, she adds as Claude turns her eye away from the bowl and towards her friend. She swears that yesterday they made this Machiavellian plan not to have lunch with her. It was a shameful dance, their guilty fingers typing short emails to each other, their wary eyes as they grabbed their handbags and then quietly put their jackets on, finally walking out, tight-lipped. They left about one minute after the other. She is no fool: they met by the lift and went for lunch without her. Giulia bites her left thumbnail, and as she looks up, Claude is staring at her and has stopped slicing the fruits, her head leaning towards her bubbly friend, who is so insecure when she has nowhere to run.

Claude grabs a cake tin. The kitchen noise irritates Giulia, the sounds exponentially louder after a long run. She can feel her heart pounding fast in her temple. Claude interrupts her thoughts, 'It sounds to me like they all went for lunch?'

'That's my point. They didn't invite me to lunch.'

'It takes time, Giulia. Also, you need to stop eating so late. Those guys were probably starving by then.'

Claude delicately builds the crumble, a layer of sugar-coated sliced apples first, the butter and flour mixture next, a sprinkle of cinnamon on top, and quietness invades the kitchen. Once her hands are clean again, she regrets her sarcasm.

'Look at how it is with you. You always get on with others. And I adore this about you, how against any fuss you are. How bloody pragmatic you can be. I really do. But I worry for you too.' Giulia drinks another sip of water and delicately puts her glass back on the counter before continuing, 'You went along with Sophie, her whims, her extravagances, for all these years, putting yourself in some pretty horrific situations, neglecting your feelings and now look where you are. Where you both are. I wish you would realise there can be some good in listening to your emotions over facts.'

How had their conversation turned into an argument about Sophie so abruptly? It is a funny one, the pace of life between two friends, how it ranges widely between laughter and tears, between compassion and judgement, accelerating from light tones to defensive punches. Claude had no intention of hurting Giulia so why is she throwing the ball back at her so aggressively? Does she not love Sophie anymore?

'I'm sorry about lunch, it sucks to be left out of something as basic as lunchtime.'

'Have you talked to Sophie recently?'

'Non,' she says, and she meant the French here. It sounds stronger in French, the extra, redundant letter causing one to dread the abrupt negativity for a little longer. *Non c'est non.* 'I'm sorry you're in the middle of this. I'm sorry we cannot go for lunch the three of us together.'

'I have always been in the middle of you two. I only used to think it was for the best when now it's really gone to shit.'

Claude smiles, she loves that Giulia swears so much.

'I'm sorry.'

'Stop apologising, Claude. Go and run to Sophie now. Speak your emotions before they eat you alive. You've got to stop feeding us and start telling us how you feel. Run to her house. I don't know, bring flowers. She loves them.' Giulia is moving fast again; Claude's flat shrinks. 'I know! Do the ridiculous cardboard message thingy from *Love Actually.*'

Claude interrupts her, 'Is she living with Allegra?'

'At Allegra's, where Allegra is a rare feature. Yes.'

The pause drags on; their eyes lock. Claude's lips open into a wistful smile. 'I can't do the messages on the cardboard. It's only cute if it's a man who does it.' Her smiles widen, welcoming her wit. 'It's regarded as pathological hysteria if a woman does it.'

The pressure in the air has significantly dropped, suddenly, releasing them both. 'I think it's pretty fucked up regardless of your gender.' Giulia is licking leftover crumble preparation from her fingers, her eyes rushing to meet Claude again.

'They're stupid, you know, to not want to go for lunch with you.'

Once Giulia is gone, Claude grabs her phone and quickly, too quickly to stop her fingers from typing, she is googling Sophie's name. There are numerous articles about her parents, fewer about her, and those still feature her parents. It upsets her, this staged life Sophie leads, despite not being the main actress. She ends up on Sophie's social media accounts, on her virtual photographic diaries. Claude is reassured to see she posted a photo of her scrambled eggs this morning. It is good that she is eating.

Giulia takes the bus back to South London. She likes to cross the Thames while sitting on the top of a double-decker bus. She took a book from Claude's library on her way out for the journey, *Nada* by Carmen Laforet. Claude recommended she meet Andrea, the teenager who runs through the streets of Barcelona, although Giulia knows deep down that she won't read further than the first page during the commute. Distractions will catch up with her first: the view, the kids playing loud music on speakers, the couple in the front row, someone will be on the phone for sure. She sends a few voice messages too, not worrying how many fragments of herself she is sharing since she is talking fast and in Italian. She listens to them again while she waits for her mother to reply and that is when she remembers, her head spinning, that there are over a hundred and thirty thousand Italians living in London, let alone however many tourists. How many could potentially be riding the same bus as her? She looks at the view, checks her phone again and then, faster than it takes for the minute hand to go around the clock, she sends these two texts to Sophie:

Ciao darling, how are you?

You should text Claude. I miss you today and so does Claude.

She reads over them a few times, even though it is too late now. Then she picks up the novel she borrowed from Claude again. Except that she cannot focus on the printed words. The messages, they are sent. Impatient, her feet tapping against the sticky lining of the floor of the bus, she flicks through the last pages of *Nada*. She wants to know where she is heading. She could delete them, the messages, but it does not take away the fact that the text box will be there in their thread, for ever, only with a *deleted* mention. What would she tell Sophie? She cannot say that she drunk texted her, it's only 3:30 p.m. She means it, though, she misses them. She cannot delete their friendships; she cannot delete their form of loving.

In November, Claude, Giulia and Sophie fail to communicate.

Claude

'We broke up. We broke up a lifelong friendship and I went through all the stages you go through after experiencing a separation. I blamed her, I blamed me, I added more blameful acts to my name, I thought I would never be able to breathe again. How tragic would that be? I pretended it didn't happen, continuing my life as it was before, but minus Sophie. I remembered that it had happened every night as my mind loosened up. It hurt constantly, but the most in the mornings when I first opened my eyes. And then I began a new journey, towards a better version of myself, moving on from the Claude of the past – becoming a future self who has learnt from her mistakes. It's exhausting, you know, this constant questioning when I do something – is that old Claude or new Claude? I went on a few runs following Giulia's advice, I drank my weight in wine some nights, I baked as if I was the only one left with flour in her pantry and needed to feed the rest of the world. But everything I did felt flat.

There was no Sophie to send a sweaty post-run selfie to, no Sophie to flush out my alcoholic excess with on the dance floor, no Sophie to eat her slice of cake – her mouth full of crumbs, hand rushing towards her lips as she bursts into laughter. She has a razor-sharp laugh and I miss that every moment, a special fragment of my Sophie. The girl with whom I walked and ran through the school corridors, the woman alongside whom I have counted all the way to one hundred hoping to defeat any obstacles life threw at us, the eyes I always found in the corner of any room I ever entered. I miss my friend above everything. There are pains in my body from the shame, stinging reminders that I am not worthy of human contact. Somehow it seems that the magnetic field around my skin does not attract others. Or that once touch has happened, the hands make the legs flee. But it is the break-up I find the hardest to overcome: Sophie broke up with me and now I must accept that there won't be a better version of myself once I reach the other side. There will be life and I will be walking through it, minus Sophie. You know what I mean? It's tough because I never dared to imagine it could happen.'

'Do you think you took Sophie for granted?'

'I think she took me for granted.'

'In what sense?'

'I don't know.' I collect myself. My palms are moist, holding my hips tight, my eyes focus on the old clock at the back of the room, my pupils still. *Tic tac tic tac tic tac.* 'She has pushed me so far over the edge that a part of me thinks she always thought I would come back. That there was no limit to hurting me because I wouldn't be strong enough to erase her from my life.' *Tac tac tac tac tic.* 'Because she knows that she makes up for my family.'

'Do you think that's true?'

'What is true?'

'That you're not strong enough to leave Sophie behind?'

'That's a surprising question. Does abandoning someone make you stronger? I always thought about it the other way around, as in having been abandoned makes me stronger.'

'When a person is toxic to your well-being, it is a valid thought to want to break up with that person. Who has abandoned you?'

'So you think Sophie is toxic?'

'Does that make you angry?'

'No. She is not toxic. She is hurting.'

'Do you struggle with your sexuality?'

'I have no issue with being queer.'

'Do your family and friends define you as a lesbian?'

'We don't speak about this with my friends because they respect my intimacy. I choose who I sleep with, who I love, and that is not their problem.'

'Do you identify as bisexual?'

'I think my identity is more complex than a question of choosing the correct word that'll define my sexual orientation.'

'Don't you think it can be empowering to identify with someone else?'

'It settles others' expectations, it serves the purpose of data collection to be able to list sexual orientations on a form, but it doesn't help me to understand how does one protect themselves when they start to feel for someone else.'

'Do you masturbate?'

'Excuse me?'

'How do you feel about your body?'

'I feel fine about it but it feels rejected.'

The therapist hums and nods.

I carry on, 'You know, rationally, my body is okay. It ticks the boxes with all the required organs and parts and it looks fine to me. I like my waistline and how long earrings frame my face. But then it often feels as if my body is not right for this world. Like do jeans ever really fit other people, both the waist size and the leg length? Because to me the disharmony is frightening. I have to choose between a belt or having to crop my trousers. And it often feels like that I guess, like somehow I have to shrink a part of myself so I can move forward. And I guess I am exhausted from the race. Well, tired, at least; I'm tired.' Claude shakes her head so her eyes meet those of the doctor, her pale pink shirt tucked into blue jeans. 'Sometimes when I close the door I fall flat against it, out of breath, feeling as if I was melting. I'm not sure what it is that I'm running away from but there is something. And then it kills me because I know what it is, I've always known. It's Sophie.'

The therapist continues to nod and, for a second, I wish

I could hug her. The clock has settled, both hour and minute hands gathering to meet in agreement at the hour.

'So yes, my best friend broke up with me and it's messing with me. Do you think I'm weak?'

'Would you say Sophie is the love of your life?'

'She is the closest person I have. Does that qualify?'

'You define your forms of love, Claude. What do you look for in love?'

'I look for someone who will simply let me be quiet by their side.'

'But then you seem to think Sophie took you for granted by doing so?'

'She let me fall behind. After we came together in Lisbon, after that one night, she stopped listening. She didn't give me a chance to explain how I felt or what I want for us. She caught me off guard.' I look away from the therapist. 'She abandoned me.'

'Do you think you put too much pressure on this one relationship?'

'If I think back now, do I think it was ludicrous to assume Sophie could be my best friend and sister and lover? It certainly does sound incestuous.'

We both surprise ourselves with a smile. I am growing tense as I wait for the therapist to mention an Oedipus complex of some sort. *Please don't. I really don't want this to turn clinical.* Her shoulders lift and her head gently turns towards the clock before she concludes: 'I'm aware of time and I do think we would benefit from having further sessions.

In the meantime, I suggest you write a letter to Sophie, just for yourself at this stage. You can bring it with you next time and read it to me. You need to find what Sophie means to you and what role she is playing in your life before you can fully break up with her. Or make amends. We love many people through the course of our lives, some for a specific amount of time and others for a lifetime. All kinds of love bring us something different but no one can make you love yourself, other than you. That's what we will try to do together, Claude, find yourself and what you love about yourself so nobody can ever take it away from you, and so you can be loved and love safely.'

I leave the room, shaken and revitalised all at once. I will walk home: it will do me good. I stop at one of the corner shops along the way, where I gift myself a bag of sweets. Those gluey, chewy blue sweets I never crave but which bring me back to my childhood days, still. I remember how much we fought to have the one with the red hat back in school – it was an affirmation of privilege within the hierarchy of children. I always gave mine to Sophie. But not today. Today, I'm walking down the street and wolfing down the sweets, the red hats first in line, swiftly, stuffing my face. They are mine.

I throw the empty bag of sweets in the bin and am submerged by a sudden rush of guilt. I feel selfish that I ate all the sweets and careless that I put my teeth at risk and anyway,

I don't even think I like these sweets. I still don't understand what it is about the red-hat Smurf. They all taste of the same chemical mixture to me. My apartment is approaching and I'm feeling anxious at the idea of closing the door behind me. It will be quiet inside. The fridge is empty and the kitchen spotless, a rare sight since I moved in. I'm frightened that nothing will ever taste the same and my ability to taste and to create new flavours for others is what I love the most about myself. It is how I find strength to put one foot in front of the other: so I can taste and make others taste. Not even the red-hat Smurf tasted different.

As I walk past the last grocery store before home, I decide that I must bake. Something decadent. Something I would have never dared to bake for Sophie. Something grotesque, like the apple green marzipan cakes in the boulangeries in France. Like the ones Kirsten Dunst devours when she plays Sofia Coppola's Marie Antoinette. 'I Want Candy' plays on repeat in my head while I launch myself along the aisles, roaming, unsure about what to make. I look at the fruits on offering but I do not like sponge cakes so it would need to be a tart. None of the fruits seem to be ripe enough for this purpose. It would not take long enough to make. I turn my eyes away when they meet a box of cornflakes. The hungry girl in me sometimes reached for the long and colourful cardboard packaging for a snack, hauling myself onto the bar stool in the kitchen, only to taste bitter smoke. Maman always grabbed a handful of cornflakes as she stepped back into our flat from the balcony after a cigarette. Washed-out, cold smoke flakes. I cringe and move on to the next aisle. I'm not a fan of chocolate cakes either and I hate to bake with chocolate bars. The texture takes the fun away from working butter and flour together. I think about making a cheesecake – she would have hated that, Sophie – but I really want to knead dough. Then I remember that I wanted to make a lemon meringue pie for my housewarming, until I found beautiful strawberries and decided to bake Sophie's favourite almond and strawberry tart. Tonight I will be having a housewarming with myself – I am, after all, going home. I grab a box of twelve eggs, for the pastry and the filling and the meringue. I choose the shiniest lemons and add limes because I like their acidity. I cannot find cream of tartar but a tablespoon of vinegar will do fine as a substitution. I cannot remember if I still have cornstarch so I buy more, and butter. I buy a bottle of red Brouilly wine because I'm having a sour celebration today. I start to walk faster, back and forth, up and down the aisles, adding random items to my basket, for the simple reason that I want to.

I open the bottle of wine first, turn the radio on because I do not want to have to decide what I will be listening to as I put the shopping away. I eye Allegra's food processor and decide against using it. I roll up my sleeves and begin to incorporate the butter and the flour until they resemble breadcrumbs. I have cold water by my side so I can slowly pour some in, while I continue to mix, until the pastry comes together. I wrap the ball in cling film and set it aside in the fridge. I drink more wine and begin to plan my next steps for the rest of the recipe. I preheat the oven and feel instantly reassured by the sound of gas. Then, I prepare my pastry for blind baking – one of my favourite things to do when I cook. I love to roll pastry, flawless movement shaping into a circle. Then fitting it into the tart tin, moulding the circle to its shell-like shape, rolling the edges. It makes me feel grounded, preparing a solid base for my tart. It seems like the easiest step in such a preparation, yet it is the most important. If the crust doesn't hold, there will be no tart. I look for pulses and blind bake until the crust turns golden. I stay still while it bakes, looking through the oven, sipping wine. The radio is moving through decades in a blitz of minutes passing. A song by Sinéad O'Connor plays and an instant smile links my cheeks together. Once the crust is ready, I let it chill and start to prepare the filling. Light-headed, air sucked from the rare oxygen in the small kitchen and my thoughts emptying. I haven't had lunch so I make a little extra to taste as I go along. I first mix together the lemon and lime zest and juice, with cornflour and water, in a saucepan. The apartment is getting warmer, the windows steamy. I add egg yolks and sugar, although cautiously for the latter because I want my pie on the bitter side. Then I whisk. I whisk vigorously until the mixture thickens. The weight on my shoulders starts to lift as I do; my head clears. I'm in control. I now melt the butter along with my fear of being alone, my hatred of the shape of my lips and the memory of Sophie's hands against my body. I set the filling aside while it cools. I then spoon it into the pastry shell and let it chill in the fridge. I'm ready – if I can produce such sweet, dedicated labour, I can date. I think about Giulia and do my best to learn from her experience. I download the app she said was her favourite, the one that made her feel human.

Connect with Facebook or phone number – who on earth would link their Facebook profile? 'Hi guys, I haven't posted since high school but you can now find me on the below dating app.' This is not starting well, I think. I pour myself another glass of wine.

Phone number. Enter verification code. You are verified.

Create account.

Why is it purple? A colour that is associated with nobility and wealth. On second thoughts, I do feel bourgeois: sipping wine, baking a lemon meringue tart, creating a dating profile so I too can be entitled to love.

Facebook pre-fill? Still a no.

What's your name? Claude. I've got this.

What's your date of birth? I let out a small, sharp laugh as I notice you can change the date later, as if I might change my mind about this lie. I enter my real date of birth. 17 July 1991.

What's your email? Now this is getting intrusive.

Never miss a message from someone great. Enable Notifications. Disable Notifications. Disable.

Are you sure? Oui oui.

Enter basic information:

Where do you live? This is getting creepy, I swear. More wine.

What's your gender? I think my therapist had an opinion about this one earlier. *Woman.*

Who do you want to date? Putain. I should have done it with her. I panic-select *Everyone.*

How tall are you? Really? I go to my cupboard and grab a tape measure. It seems to be the most important detail I can share right now – the one piece of information about myself that feels the truest – a new objective knowledge about my person. I grab a pencil and stand against my kitchen wall, like we did once a year during the school's medical visit. Sophie trembled as she waited for the nurse to weigh her on the tall scale, the red arrow jumping right as we stepped up, a ticking box for how good we looked, us hungry girls. She then had to say the figure out loud, in front of an audience of twenty-plus pupils, for the secretary to enter the data in her notebook. I try to be precise. I discover that I measure 1 metre 66. I like that.

What's your ethnicity? What about children? What's your hometown? Where do you work? What's your job title? Well, you tell me.

Where did you go to school? What's the highest level you attained? Now the colour purple does make sense. *What are your religious beliefs? What are your political beliefs? Do you drink? Do you smoke? Do you smoke weed?* What kind of idiot says yes to this? *Do you use drugs?* This is getting hilarious now.

I am exhausted and my tart filling is nowhere near chilled enough. I open a bag of crisps and move on to creating my profile. I need photos. Right, I have got this. I begin to scroll down my gallery but I close it fast — it holds too many memories and I do not want to turn sour for my public profile. The tart is enough. I quickly select a selfie I took last week after I bought flowers and a picture Sophie took of me in Lisbon. Now I need to select prompts. OK, this is fun.

A shower thought I recently had — is it more sustainable to turn off the heating during the day or to leave it on constantly but at a lower temperature?

The one thing you should know about me is — I like to bake.

My biggest date fail — sleeping with my best friend.

Biggest risk I've taken — baking lemon meringue pie as I drink alone in my kitchen. And creating a profile on this app. At the same time.

Dating me is like — an avant-première.

We're the same type of weird if — you are in love with your best friend, waited ten years, slept with them and then never spoke to them again.

This is going nowhere. The pie is looking good. I begin to make the meringue, which involves me whisking more eggs, but I've grown tired. I wet the sugar and it reminds me of the shoreline in France. I wonder what would have happened to Maman if dating apps existed in her time — would she have found a shoulder to rest her head on? Would a shoulder have been enough to bring her balance and keep her in our home? I must focus on the meringue. Was I not enough? I bring the sugar to a boil and leave it to simmer. I do my best to beat the egg whites so they form a soft peak, and then I continue to beat, faster and faster, as I pour in the hot sugar. I continue to whisk until cool, quiet tears run down my cheeks. Was I not enough for Maman to want to taste life? I fold through the vinegar and breathe deeply for a minute. I finish my glass of wine and then I spoon the meringue on top of the filling. I brown it under the grill. What should I have done differently to be a better daughter? I cut through my most beautiful creation to date with a wet knife and resume my dating profile.

Winter

1

Allegra was hit by a bus on the morning of 3 December 2019. It happened fast. A witness said she slipped on ice, sliding straight onto Tottenham Court Road. Obituaries flooded in, mostly testifying to Allegra's assiduity, creativity and patrimony. She had first entered the Vogue House press rooms via the sharpness of her pen. She had won an essay competition with a piece about her mother's tailored jacket and how it failed to suit her lines. It launched her career, dedicated to freeing women from menswear, each magazine issue she directed featuring models on glossy covers but reshaping the vests, the jeans and the suits they had been denied for years. Allegra was proud to remind everyone who questioned her journey that she was runner and then an intern, making tea, picking up dress pins, and that it took two years for anyone to call her Allegra. As her legacy portrays a memorable past, few words paint her family. *Allegra leaves behind her daughter, Sophie Cruwys, who also works in the fashion industry, and her grieving husband, designer Mark Cruwys.*

Family and distant friends of Allegra attended the funeral. Sophie and her friends reunite afterwards, seeking refuge among the constant muddling at the pub, words failing them. As if Allegra was there, sipping her Martini at the bar, watching them quietly, circling her manicured fingers around the coaster.

Sophie exhales loudly and then mutters, almost inaudibly, 'Tragic.'

Giulia tucks her hair back behind her ears: 'To be fair, she always was dramatic, Allegra.'

The silence falls back, heavier than before, their grief palpable. Giulia, who normally has no skill in reading a room correctly, tries her hardest not to bring her hand to her mouth in apology. Then Sophie bursts into loud, contagious laughter.

'She bloody was,' she snorts.

They all follow, holding their stomachs; blowing their noses and wiping away their tears next. And so they begin their own obituary of Allegra: the diet of roasted almonds, cigarettes and Diet Coke; the blunt-cut bob, trembling hands despite the effort she put into hiding them; the day she found Sophie's weed stash in her teenage bedroom, her warm and musky perfume; how everything was either *h-o-rri-fic* or *char-ming;* how much she adored the colour orange; the movement her hips made each time the music of Billie Holiday played in the background.

When she first heard, Giulia called Claude, just a few seconds after she hung up with Sophie, in tears, devastated. No one had imagined something would dare hit Allegra. Claude did not think twice, of course she was coming to the funeral. She texted Sophie to check if she was comfortable having her around, asked if she needed anything, with shy, few words. Sophie replied with a simple '*Toi.*' She meant the French, an invitation for her friend to accompany her in counting to one hundred again, all the way to *cent*. Dean joined them too, along with their old friends from university. They had all met Allegra along the years, briefly or more extensively, at their graduation and birthday parties. Sophie had criticised her mother openly over the same years, claiming she did not have a mother at times, crying about how selfish she was, but there was no doubt that Sophie respected Allegra. Her dedication to empowering women with matching outfits is one Sophie had carried through into her ambition as a make-up artist. She points out when her skirt has pockets, always with a proud nod to Allegra. They all came for Sophie today.

'Does anyone know how to draw a rabbit?' Sophie asks the friends, who are grouped together around a round table, high velvet sofas holding their backs straight after a long and tiring day.

There is a noticeable pause before Claude replies, 'A rabbit? I can try if you want.'

'Allegra and I, we used to draw bunnies together. She was a really good artist and I was obsessed with rabbits when I was a kid. We had lots of them: Oscar, Moustache, Caramel.' The friends' eyes turn red at the thought of Allegra giving silly names to pets with her daughter. Sophie composes herself, aligning her fringe with her slim eyebrows. She wears delicate grey pearls on her ears, which she found in Allegra's jewellery box earlier this morning. 'Each time one of them died, we sat together and drew a bunny in their memory. We made a little shrine in the corner of our pantry. My nanny was freaked out by it but we loved this private corner of ours. You know, they were the small rabbits, the ones with the droopy ears. They have such fragile hearts.' Sophie's hand brushes pillings away from her woollen scarf. She concludes, 'They die young.'

Dean reaches out to take Sophie's hand; their fingers don't entwine. He did not know and can see from the look on her face that neither did Claude. Nick clears his throat and begins to talk: 'When Dad left us, it helped me to write him letters. I was young so they were childish, you know, a lot of comments about what I ate and how I was going to seek revenge on any kid who bothered me at school, or who was more brilliant.' He stops for a second, recollecting his thoughts, taking the time to consider each word. 'I still do it, for small and big life events, present and past. I introduce him to the new people in my life I wish he knew, also. I recently came out to him in a letter. My words were calm after years of failed drafts. I was angry because he denied seeing how and who I loved for years. But I want to love and I had to tell him.' Dean slips his hand away from Sophie's, his gaze turning towards the pub's monumental wooden door. Nick gently nods to Sophie before continuing, 'I'm not saying it was easier to open up with someone who is dead. In some ways it was harder because I won't receive any acknowledgement back from him. What I'm trying to say is that I had to break away from the assumptions I had created about him so I could find my voice. A voice that is mine even when nobody is listening, even when there is nobody to convince.'

Sophie embraces Nick tenderly and for a second it is as if everyone else has left the room, almost as if Allegra did not die earlier this week. Sophie and Nick shared modules at university, often teaming up together for finals and group projects. They rehearsed in Allegra's house, craving space and clean walls so the lighting would make their creations shine brighter. Allegra adored Nick, ever since he came to their house with a huge bouquet of orange tulips. He stayed for dinner. They shared the same stubbornness and determination when they needed to get a job done. They were both doers and Sophie always envied this quality of theirs: the ambition that drove them forward in life, when she struggles to reach the finishing line with her projects, always questioning what might be the best way instead of forging her own path, guided by her instincts. She sighs and asks, 'Are you guys up for another drink or would you rather go home?'

'Happy either way,' replies Claude.

Sophie can't stop a small smile appearing in the corner of her mouth. She has always loved the way Claude pronounces ei*th*er, reminiscent of her mother's tongue.

'Let's have another one,' and so Sophie and Claude step up towards the bar.

'You know she respected you,' says Sophie as the bartender prepares their order.

Claude nods. Sophie continues: 'I think she was grateful to you for picking me up when she failed to do so. And she felt threatened by this, too. She was concerned that I loved you more than I loved her.'

Claude has learnt that there are many forms of love, all different in their meaning, duration and painfulness. She knows that feelings flow but words are sealed with a meaning, and that most people only have words for weapons because they define and set in stone. Until today, Claude has not said a word to Sophie since Lisbon, respecting her friend's demand. The silence that has occupied the space between their lives, leaving room for interpretation, the void, the echo chamber of their friendship, has been agonising.

'How are you, Sophie?'

'I feel as if the ground has turned into water.'

Claude's hand reaches gingerly towards Sophie's back, their first touch in months. The past months are the first time in years they have stayed apart for more than a handful of days. They both shiver, feeling at home and in foreign territory. The same estranged, bittersweet sentiment one returns to when coming home after a long holiday: the comfort in knowing which key fits in the lock straight away and yet the disappointment in discovering that it is not as ideal as remembered on the journey back. A life has ended since the last time they embraced one another and, in retrospect, it feels as long as a lifetime ago. Claude is desperate to make a comment about Nick's suggestion for Sophie to write Allegra a letter, to invite Sophie to share such a letter with her. She is crafting her form of correspondence too; she has written drafts of her letter to Sophie, she could have added. But she taps her card against the reader instead. 'I owe one to Allegra.' Claude winks and her body quivers.

They carry the drinks back to the table, welcomed by their friends' wary eyes and prudent smiles.

'So . . . is everyone registered to vote?'

Jane slaps Nathan's lap. 'Nath, Allegra just . . .' She doesn't finish her sentence.

'I'm sorry,' Nathan adds, genuine regret in his eyes. He meant well: the country is in the middle of one of the most important elections in their lifetime. He is convinced of this, thus making voting a relevant topic to move their conversation towards the future. Nathan is lucky enough not to have buried anyone close to his heart before. He simply does not understand that a future without that one person who keeps one rooted is more daunting than the thought of millions of people walking towards polling stations. In the latter there is a crowd but to grieve is a lonely process. Sophie reassures Nathan, there is no trouble and Allegra would have liked them all to vote, maintaining a polite rather than convincing smile. The friends nod in response, and allow themselves to fall back into the sofa, separating in smaller groups, chatting, sharing plans for the Christmas holiday ahead, worries about the upcoming elections, anger for Giulia who is unable to vote when this election will impact her prospects in this country, surprise that Teddy can vote with his Australian passport. All debates are silenced, though, as soon as Candice asks, good-heartedly: 'Claude, how is Ciara?'

Giulia hides behind her glass of wine, electrifying curls give her secret away. She has not told Sophie that Claude is dating Ciara.

'Well. She is away, working on a new project in the Lake District.' She takes another sip of wine before she adds, 'She is a conservation biologist.'

Candice continues, to Claude's exasperation. She likes to speak about Ciara but she hates to see Sophie turning paler, drinking faster, looking frailer. 'How fun. Is she likely to relocate?'

'Not full-time but she will visit often. Anyhow, I'm going up there this weekend.'

Sophie downs her drink but most of the room is misdiagnosing her pain: it is not her mother she is mourning in this moment, and she is unsure if she can grieve twice on the same day.

2

The first time Claude met Ciara, it was outside Kew Gardens. Prior to that, they connected online, Ciara sending the first message: I believe that wearing handmade jumpers is the most sustainable choice. Claude felt inclined to engage with this stranger, who had not liked her photo but her shower thought. This in itself felt sustainable to her timid self. From her online profile, she could see that Ciara lived in Peckham, liked to go for long walks, was 'addicted' to podcasts and invited others to send her recommendations. She works for the Wildlife Trust and is dedicated to the greater cause: she is researching ways to preserve bird species at risk of extinction. Claude considered sending Ciara a podcast she enjoys, but she feared the ones she is subscribed to are not so interesting, lots of jovial chatters around tables on the topic of food. Ciara looks like the type who listens to podcasts that are reviewed as *thought-provoking*. However, Claude could argue that all conversations and arguments will trigger thoughts, not only the ones the reviewers from the *Financial Times'* Life & Art supplement had in mind when they wrote their column. She had already spent over twenty minutes thinking about what to reply to this woman, whose five photographs portrayed her as smiley and dynamic and with a fun group of friends, when she settled for an obvious question in response: Do you knit?

Ciara replied within minutes: If you don't like your jumpers with sleeves, I do.

Next, effortlessly, Claude found herself texting Ciara about jumpers and arms and global warming until the early hours of the next morning. None of the messages were longer than a sentence and most of them extracted a quick, sharp laugh from her. Each time, she hoped Ciara was doing the same on the other side of the line, and she grew curious about the woman behind the witty texts and scattered emojis. They agreed to meet the following Saturday.

Claude was wearing her favourite black trousers and shirt, but she left the top three buttons undone. She had accessorised with a pair of yellow earrings. Ciara was standing by the ticket office, dressed in high-rise mom-fit navy jeans, a simple white shirt tucked in, and the brightest of smiles. She had piercings from lobe to tip, on one ear only, with a discreet slim ring on her left nostril. Claude was intimidated by the energy that emanated from Ciara's body at first and slid her hands against her hips, anxious that she would come across as meek. Ciara hugged her quickly but tightly before she began to talk, showing Claude a leaflet.

'I picked up our tickets. They have over fifty thousand plants. Mad, eh?'

They smiled and started walking along the paths to the

gardens, continuing to review the plants, their eyes rarely meeting, their gestures timid.

'They also have a botanic garden in Sussex. Wakehurst, with woodlands and an actual nature reserve. We can go one day, and even do some birdwatching.'

Claude stayed silent, her left leg sliding, shifting her body away from Ciara. *One day* is not a quantifiable time measure from today: it evokes a future and they had only just met. This gave Claude a slight feeling of vertigo before Ciara's smile rescued her, 'You probably think birdwatching is a dull prospect for a date. Fair enough.'

Claude surprised herself as she touched Ciara's shoulder, 'Not at all. I'm a baker, you should know that I make a mess when I craft so I'll scare the birds away. But if you're all right with that, then I'm game.'

Ciara nodded. 'I first went birdwatching with my father. I grew up in a small town near Durham, my mother is a teacher and my father loves to walk. I mean, he puts bread on the table with his job too, bless him. But what he loves to do and what I love about him is going for walks. We would leave first thing in the morning while my younger siblings loved to sleep late. We walked all day, stopping along the way to look at the plants and the trees, and to listen to the birds. You can probably guess what I wrote in my personal statement when I registered for university now.' Ciara paused briefly. 'And yes, I adore my father. He has the sharpest mind I know but at the same time he is so tender. He walks at a slow pace because, and I quote him, he does it for the environment and not for the fitness. He has taught me to pause and to look around before moving on.' She hung back, dimples in her cheeks, looking downward, 'Enough about my father.'

They laughed for the first time together.

'I think I love the trees the most. I like plants, but I love trees. They are unapologetic.'

Ciara stopped and looked back towards Claude. 'I've never heard anyone using this word to define trees before.' She repeated slowly, in a mutter to herself: 'Unapologetic.'

'They group together, they grow higher so they can expand in the air, and they take so much space underground too, rooting for themselves. And then when the wind blows, they dispatch little fragments of themselves kilometres away. They are unapologetic for their being and their surviving. I'm envious. I love trees.'

'I love that you love trees. They're the home for the birds I research. In a sense, they are overlooked since we, as humans, categorise trees as unfeeling vegetation. There are many movements to save endangered species, like my birds, because they are breathing animals. Trees do breathe and more importantly they allow us to breathe. We should take better care of them.'

They took a turn towards the arboretum. A silence settled between both their bodies, the scale of the world, its state and their helplessness within it settling on them. 'Isn't it one of the best solutions for our planet, to plant more trees?' Claude asked, earnestly.

'You're right. Many researchers are arguing that planting

trees is the fastest and cheapest way to tackle the climate crisis, mostly because they clean CO_2 out of the atmosphere. It's a wonderful idea, of course it is, but I worry this discourse is making governments lazy. It's not up to trees to clean our air, it is up to governments and companies to revise how they produce and consume wealth. Trees cannot clean our past and future mess.'

'I find it difficult not to feel guilty each time I do something I enjoy. You know, do I need to board a plane to go on holiday and do I need to get this delivered to my house and do I really want an avocado?' Claude confessed, staring upward at the top of the trees. Then she added: 'I didn't cycle to meet you today because I worried I would have sweated way too much considering the distance, but at the same time, I hate that I didn't.'

'You aren't unapologetic for sure.' Claude shook her head in disbelief. Ciara continued, 'Would you like to pay a visit to the old man?'

'Your father?'

Ciara burst into laughter and Claude realised she had beautiful green eyes. 'That's a little fast, don't you think?'

Claude blushed and Ciara gently brushed her elbow against Claude's arm.

'I meant the Japanese pagoda tree. This badass comes all the way from the eighteenth century. Come on, let's go see him.'

Claude's eyes and smile widened. They walked forward.

Sophie doesn't need to check the time: she already knows that the clock reads 3 a.m. Saturday. Her nanny once told her, 'It's witching hour, darling Sophie, the time when witches are at their strongest.' Three o'clock in the morning is when nightmares made of spiders threading over her sleeping body wake Sophie. Her bones crack at the memory; is she witching or is she being bewitched? There are the nights when Sophie is heading up an army of spiders in her mind, but there also are the nights when she is up against an army of them. The latter scenario recurs most often. They run through her mouth, sliding inside her veins, popping her cells. She walks down the stairs and sighs as she feels the ice-cold flooring of the kitchen under her feet. Her ritual then begins: pouring herself a first glass of water, counting, drinking again, continuing to count, all the way to one hundred. She considers texting Claude to thank her for coming today, for ordering her a cab home. To ask her about Ciara. She cannot quite believe that Claude registered for a dating app, she who constantly leaves her phone behind. How did they speak enough to arrange a first encounter?

Sophie, who thought she could master her life, heterosexuality and norms, in the same way she orchestrates her career and work, is woken up every day at 3 o'clock in the morning by an army of spiders. She begins to type a message. She stops. Resumes. Stops again. She keeps their conversation thread open, saddened by the absence of messages from the last few months, frightened by the long silence they let settle between their lives. Her heart warms up at the thought that perhaps Claude is doing the same on the other side of this ghostly stream. If only she could see the 'online' reassuring nod appear! She would feel her presence then, she would know she is being bewitched by Claude, and that would be all right. She drinks the last drop of cold water; the spiders evaporate. She walks back to bed, her phone rests on the pillow next to her, open to her conversation with Claude.

When Claude finally appears online, Sophie is fast asleep.

4

Claude arrives at the train station early enough to buy snacks, a ceremonial ritual. When she travels, she does not care about the 3-for-2 offer, finding pride in going against her pragmatic self. She buys a disharmonious bag of snacks, widely ranging between savoury and sweet, then she heads to the vending machines, picks up her ticket, and finally sets herself up on the train. Backward facing, window seat. She spreads the goods out along with the newspaper she bought at the till, excited at the prospect of eating throughout the journey, all the way to the Lake District. Yet, as every single time she travels, she finishes her snacks before the train has time to pass the border between London's zones 2 and 3. There is nothing she can do about it: she has tried not to spread all the snacks on the table at once, to buy more, to buy less, to eat the ones she prefers first, nothing works. On the train, she is only able to wolf down her food, the self-control that others admire in her disappearing. She eats in a frenzy and scrolls through the latest world news, thriving on the buzz, her stomach too slow to process the food, her fingers shaking. But it is not long before she starts to feel an extreme sadness, a sapping guilt. And as the trees fly past the window, she feels a sense of self-reflection — perhaps triggered by the snacks that are gone, the state of the world as depicted in the newspaper – but she yearns for another form of herself. Impulsive and compulsive, alive and living, and not the considerate Claude who is waiting for life to catch her up, her days following the same routine as always. She wants to live a life she loves and not one that will make her feel loved.

Once she has swallowed her last stuffed olive, she grabs her phone out of habit and before her brain can catch up with the triggered blue ticks on her screen, she has texted Sophie. Hey, guess what? I ate all my snacks before the train left London. Every single time.

After she saw Sophie at Allegra's funeral, they texted briefly, until they started talking on the phone every day, never for too long but continuously.

Later, when her eyes cannot focus on reading anymore, she texts Ciara. On my way and I cannot wait to see you xxx

What's up with you?

What do you mean?

That's un-Claude of you.

To miss you?

I hope not. But to say so, yes.

Working on it.

I like that. Can't wait to see you too.

Claude stops replying and Ciara texts again a few minutes later. I'm coming to pick you up at the station.

She does not reply. Claude is on the phone with Sophie.

'I'm going back to work next week. I think it will be good to distract my mind, you know, to keep myself busy. The team has been great but I do need to run my business. It's going well. We're booked to do the models' make-up for a few fashion shows next year in London.' There is a short pause, 'and Paris and Milan.'

'I'm happy for you, Soph.'

'So, from a dating app to the Lake District? Come on then, tell me more.'

'Ah, that does sound quite mad. I'm happy. You know, I like her scientific mind.'

'I bet she has good survival skills like you do. What's her name again?'

Claude knows that Sophie remembers. 'Ciara, her name is Ciara.'

'Lovely. Juddy tells me I should also register with one of these apps.'

'The questions are dreadful. Like, who cares about the last thought you had in the shower? And everyone has either gone to Oxford or LSE. I'm so confused – like, why there are so many universities in this country if nobody attends them?' Claude's voice flows. 'Also, they all do the same bloody things on Sundays, a cycle along the canal and then drink a pint of fresh ale by the water.'

Claude rarely curses.

A sharp laugh escapes Sophie before she says, with a graver tone to her voice, 'I don't know how to cycle.'

'You know what they say,' there is a small silence, during which they each listen to the pattern of the other's breathing, 'it's something you never forget. It might be worth learning how to cycle now.'

'I missed you, Clo.'

'Me too.' Then silence. 'I'd better go now.'

'Sure. Safe travels and I hope to meet Ciara soon.'

Ciara is passionate and opinionated while respectful of others' opinions – something that feels rare in a person nowadays. When Claude mentioned Ciara for the first time, Giulia told her *to go for it*, because she had nothing to lose. It was the exact same advice Claude had given her back in the day, she reminded Claude, threatening to call her a hypocrite if she were to flake. Claude wonders if one day she will be brave enough to tell Ciara the truth, that she most often texted her via Giulia rather than directly, at least at the very beginning. She assumes she has guessed by now. Claude was challenged by Ciara when they started dating, especially to find her pace when they went for walks together. She realised that she wasn't used to walking alongside someone she doesn't know, and that most of the time one's pace suits the way one speaks. It took her some time to get used to Ciara's lexicon as well, to understand when she was sarcastic, when she was showing genuine interest, when she meant for her to stay and not to go home. They spent hours walking through London together, stopping for coffee and at garden centres along the way. Ciara knows the names of all the plants on offer, or at least it seems like she does in Claude's eyes, who adores this skill of hers. She picked hairy bittercress and dandelions along pathways and embankments to make broth and curries, to Claude's astonishment, the child of suburban cement. Then came the day when Claude had to allow Ciara into the intimacy of her home, and so she decided to do what she does best: Claude cooked Ciara a meal. She had Giulia on speaker while she prepared everything in the kitchen, only so she would not drink the bottle of wine before her guest arrived. She was not worried about cooking a lemon sole; on the other hand, her stomach was upside down at the prospect of having a new woman walk into the yellow kitchen. *What will she think of the green bathroom? Probably that I have no taste.* Claude agonised; Giulia brushed her off. Claude was grateful for this, back then. She and Ciara get along, the sex is good and they are taking their journey together one step at a time, leaving space for the other to pursue their own schedules. So why is she suddenly panicking at the prospect of her train entering the station in Oxenholme this morning? She should feel excitement. Butterflies in her stomach, so they say, no? She does not feel capable of giving Ciara love, instead she selfishly feasts on Ciara's love. She takes the love but does not love back. She hates this about their relationship, the harsh realisation of their dynamics now that they are past the first discoveries and are moving on to the quietness of togetherness. Claude fears the person she is becoming alongside Ciara, a feeling of dependence disrupting a lifetime of individualism, letting the expectations she set for herself loosen up. It started with small clues, when she forgot to buy eggs for instance, then the smell of Ciara pervaded her bedsheets and now she realises how much time has stretched since she baked something new. The train manager announces the next station is approaching. Ciara stands on the platform, with red mittens, an umbrella hanging at the end of her left hand, the clouds emerge low and thick.

They fight vigorously but only for a few minutes.

'You cannot put words in my mouth,' claims Ciara. Her knees surge, as sharp as a skeleton's, her eyes rebel with shades of red. 'If you're freaking out, at least be honest with me,' she spits.

Claude stays silent, her mouth closed and eyes dry. She has announced she is not good enough for Ciara, that she could not give her what she wants and that she is so grateful to her, and for what she has taught her about herself. Ciara has learnt from Claude that not everything is defined by scientific facts, some truths are determined under the remit of one's subjectiveness. She had assumed she understood Claude, she regrets this now. Claude has grown to trust that not all forms of love lead to abandonment, that her body does not make everyone that touches it run away, and some might even desire to touch her again. She misses being a person of her own, she concludes. They exchange a final, tender and quiet smile before Claude books herself onto an earlier train to London.

In the rush of running away, Claude forgets to buy snacks.

★ ★ ★

When Claude opens the door of the yellow kitchen again, she is struck by the signs of her aloneness she left behind. The smallest Moka pot she owns stands on the hob, a single plate on the drying rack. On the counter, the fruit bowl lingers half-empty, a butternut squash destined for rotting lies against its wooden sides. Alone in her kitchen, Claude cuts the squash in two, massages it with oil, salt and pepper and knits together sprigs of thyme and rosemary to add on top. This last ode to autumn in the form of a vegetable disappears into the oven, the warming wind from the machine gives back colour to Claude's fingers and nose. She is cooking a dinner for one. Butternut squash gnocchi with a butter and sage sauce. The dough she must work before she can serve dinner; the warming butter for Maman and Mamie, the golden evaporating bubble and ubiquitous smell it creates; sage, her winter mint.

As she waits for the squash to bake, Claude reorganises her kitchen. She brings her favourite cups and the smaller saucepans forward at the front of the shelves. She sorts out her spices: oregano, turmeric, cumin seeds, chilli flakes and black pepper stay near the hob; nutmeg, Tabasco, smoked paprika and ground ginger are put away in the cupboards. She counts her bags of flour and dreams of buying voluminous glass jars so she can store the explosive powders properly. She knows already that she won't indulge this wish; she seals each bag cautiously with pins instead. Claude keeps the 00 flour out and begins to pass the vegetable's flesh through a sieve. This is hard work that requires her muscles to pull, her brain to pause as its focus turns to the synergy between her arms and hands, far from the rest, the flesh left behind to dry, the gurgle of draining water last. *He was mastered by the sheer surging of life, the tidal wave of being, the perfect joy of each separate muscle, joint and sinew in that it was everything that was not death, that it was aglow and rampant, expressing itself in a movement, flying exultantly under the stars and over the face of dead matter that did not move,* Maman murmurs. Claude reaches for a bowl next, adds the squash and mixes in flour, one egg and shaved parmesan. The broken shell leaves her fingers sticky. She seasons the dough with salt and pepper. She grins as she remembers she should add nutmeg and returns to the sliding cupboard to seize the spice, a nod to Giulia. She kneads the dough on a floured surface, divides it into four pieces and rolls each one of them into a log, dough residues stick to her hands like limpets on beach rocks. She cuts the gnocchi into two-centimetre pieces and rolls each gnocco against the back of her fork. She turns the radio on halfway through the process. A smile plays across her lips as her thumb rolls against the channel knob, as she allows herself to search for a new station, one of her choice, alone at home. She pursues each gnocco meticulously as her hands work to make something good for herself after today's journey. She sets one batch of gnocchi aside and puts the leftovers in the freezer. There will be future dinners for one. For now, she boils the balls of pasta in salted water until they float to the surface. The dough holds together, the gnocchi swim back up, and so she lights up the gas on the next hob, the sage crisps and the butter bubbles before she coats each gnocco in the thick sauce. She plates her gnocchi, a top-up of shaved parmesan, and so Claude eats at the wobbly, wooden table.

The yellow walls stand for the full moon.

5

Sophie appears through the door of the Soho pub, wrapped up in a long fur coat and an oversized woollen scarf. She looks concerned at first, her brain switching from the after-work, fast-paced walk from Covent Garden to Soho, among the men in suits drinking on the pavements, to the noise bouncing back against the pub's walls. Her face quickly lights up as she sees Claude and Giulia, standing in a corner, a bottle of red wine between them. There is an extra, unused glass too. They are expecting her.

As they do every year since they left university, Jane and Nathan have organised their annual Christmas reunion, which seems to take place earlier every year. They dread it and they still have fun. Finally, the evening turns sour when the time arrives to open the Secret Santa gifts, a ceremony that has become more and more about who is the most successful, the best at buying gifts. Giulia roars harder than ever when they do not even have dinner for a Christmas do – 'the most antithetical party,' she claims. They worry they might feel like strangers before they arrive, yet they soon realise not much has changed. Most of them remain truthful to who they were expected to become.

'I'm so cold these days,' Sophie announces as she hugs her friends hello.

'Still not cold enough to justify the number of rabbits you killed to make that new coat of yours.' Sophie receives the critique like a judgemental needle, her eyebrows thicken. Claude goes pale. 'I'm so sorry, Soph. The rabbits, of course you wouldn't want to mistreat rabbits. I should have thought twice before I spoke.' She pauses. 'I'm sorry.'

'That's all right. Speaking of wildlife, have you brought Ciara with you tonight?'

'We broke up.'

Giulia hands Sophie a glass of red, 'Finest house Merlot for you, my darling. Things are a little tight with the Christmas holidays ahead of us,' she adds, keen to move away from wild and intimate lives equally, switching their focus back to bigger problems. Capitalism seems sizeable enough.

Sophie raises her glass, 'Well, in this case, me too: I'm sorry.' Her eyes pierce into Claude's wide, round pupils. 'Cheers. And a merry Christmas to you both.'

Their glasses meet and so the evening starts. Tonight is the first time they are reunited for an evening together since Allegra's funeral. They exchanged dates, all falling flat, all of them busy with other projects, switching their priorities. Giulia is the one who grows nostalgic on the edge of the first glass of wine's last drop. 'I missed having you two in the same room. It feels right, don't you think? I bet if there was a movie about us, it wouldn't feature any men.'

Claude gently knocks her friend's shoulder with hers, 'I see no men here. Never have.'

'It bothers me.'

There is a short second of readjustment as they realise that Giulia is not joking, she is confessing a secret to her best friends: 'I said it. It kills me.'

'What are you saying?'

'That I love men.'

'Fair enough,' Claude adds with a tight smile, wary eyes rolling towards Sophie.

Giulia plays with her fingernails. 'I'm bringing Teddy with me to Italy for the holidays this year, so I can introduce him to my family.' Her voice breaks into an unfamiliar rhythm, her eyes meet both her friends' before she refocuses on the tip of her thumb. 'I guess I'm afraid to lose you.'

Sophie clears her throat. 'But Juddy, we're not going anywhere. We'll be the ones picking up the pieces when he messes up.' An open smile lights up her face as she adds: 'And if we ever get to that stage, I know of a fabulous apartment in Lisbon for us.'

Giulia grabs Sophie's hand in return, 'Fair enough,' she adds.

Claude looks back and forth between these two women she loves so deeply. She has surprised herself over the last few months: meeting new people, having casual conversations with strangers, dating, speaking up about her opinions, disagreeing, even when it might be a bother to others. She has applied for a scholarship to pursue a baking traineeship, half to prove to herself that she could step up for herself, for her own good, half because she believes she is a good enough baker. She let the deadline threateningly close in until she finally opened the Word document and started typing, her fingers moving fast before her as she realised that this is what she wants. She bloomed as she filled in the application, as she did something to make herself shine and as it did not make her a worse friend, nor a worse daughter. She did not think it would lead to anything concrete, either. The website was clear about the competitive nature of the application process: they only accepted ten candidates and received hundreds of applications from all around the world. She decided not to alarm anyone so she kept her registration a secret, until a letter came back. It was short and sweet – a delightful acceptance to join a chef traineeship in Rome, for just six months. A good start, she concluded as she contemplated the letter, slowly realising that what will come next will be up to her. She was excited and she suddenly understood what Giulia meant when she spoke about why she ran so much. *It's about the lightness of being, Claude. When you know you're making something happen for yourself, this feeling of control over your own empowerment, one step at a time.* She felt exactly this when she opened the letter. Lightness and being. Freedom is a muscle one must exercise for oneself. Nothing else mattered; no one could have changed Claude's mind: she was going to Rome to train as a baker.

She puts her glass of wine down before she announces, matter-of-factly, happily: 'I'm moving to Rome at the end of December, for a few months.'

Giulia and Sophie look shocked, but Claude jumps in before they try to speak. 'I was granted a scholarship at a baking school there. I'll be learning from the best pastry chefs, gaining some experience at their restaurants and bakeries. I'll be spending some time on my own, doing what I always wanted to do.' There is a silence until she adds, 'The yellow kitchen is going on the road,' her usual yellow earrings moving up along with her cheeks as her widest smile comes through.

Sophie's body freezes, her brain processing the news, her mind counting how many eggshells have been broken since she has known Claude. It is Giulia who rushes to Claude first, spilling some of her wine along the way, 'Oh Claude, Roma is so lucky to have you.' She is now embracing her friend tightly. Sophie joins them in hugging and finally they have arrived home, in their friendship, this harbour of shared female intimacy. The night goes on as they drink and dance. The moon appears and streetlights lead the way, Claude heads north, Sophie goes west and Giulia crosses the river south, like three magnetic forces. Opposite poles attract each other; similar poles repel. The seasons change colours before them, verbs conjugate in the future tense, planet Earth acts as a magnet.

As 2019 draws to an end, Claude, Giulia and Sophie have learnt to coexist in their friendship, freed from the fear of each other's eyes, gracefully accepting their different choices and beliefs.

Giulia

Time is your secret ingredient. Marija and Nonna, their constant meandering around the house and the streets of Bologna, made these few words our family leitmotif. Marija's hasty footsteps pushed her body to move faster than her shadow, a fugitive running between work shifts, household chores and shops. Nonna waited for me behind the school's high, rusty gates made of wrought iron, her long pencil skirt and hands tightened closely in front of her, a piadina sandwich wrapped up in kitchen towels inside her bag. We shared the flatbread as we walked back home, a slice of prosciutto and shaved fontina cuddled in the middle, the account of my day's achievements for tempo. She sends me a parcel every two months, reminders of how long I have been gone, welcome smells and tastes from home. This month's box included pancetta because in winter, I should be making ragù and freezing extra portions for the rainy days, the handwritten note instructed.

215

They are getting harder to read with time, Nonna's arthritis disturbs the curves of her letters, the nostalgia of her life narrows her eyesight and causes her to return to the dialect more often, a language I do not read or speak. The recipe for her ragù, however, is one I can follow with my eyes closed, guided by the sound of her and Marija arguing about meat cooking methods and timings, about desalting, the jaunty sound of a sauce that simmers and reunites our family at the end of the day. I invited Teddy to come over for dinner tonight, the first time I'll cook something for him on my own, not a takeaway, nor a quick fix we put together, coming back from the pub light-headed. Tagliatelle con ragù alla Bolognese.

I started the ragù early in the afternoon. I toyed with the idea of calling Marija and my grandmother so we could cook together, but I can't handle the thought of seeing them working in a pair while I stand alone in front of the fridge. My flatmates will be roaming around the kitchen, no doubt, dropping in with clumsy memories of Italian words and food from their holidays. I am the one cooking for Teddy today, so I set things in motion with a soffritto. One carrot, one celery, a red onion and parsley, each I thinly chop. I toss the skin and leaves from the carrot and celery, the parsley stems and onion skin into a separate pan, and bring them to the boil with the intention of making broth. I cook the meat separately and set it aside. I return to my soffritto and add a generous splash of red wine. I pulse the fire and wait until the smell of alcohol has disappeared. My hips start to move from one side to another, slowly, encouraged by the frizzling soffritto before me. The evaporating alcohol reminds me of London nightclubs, their sticky floors and my energised dancing feet. We feared alcohol in my household as it alters vision, blurs dictation and mellows violence. Marija's regimen, one glass for cheer, two drops for the devil's tears. One family rule I have broken. I reach for a small pack of dried porcini mushrooms next, a pair of scissors and I am running down the Apennine hills. Emilia Romagna, the land of white truffles and mushrooms, the plains and river Po, the dishes that taste of earth and the products its soil grants us. I add the mushrooms to the pot, two cans of tomatoes, the broth and a splash of tomato purée. A good stir. I add the meat, cover and leave the ragù to simmer on a low heat for the rest of the afternoon. Time is my secret ingredient.

Teddy arrives. He looks composed, and has the appearance of someone who is about to walk into an unknown room with framed photos, signs of memories that are both inviting and foreign. He has brought a bottle of red wine, Shiraz, which he unscrews as I walk towards the cupboards and come back with two glasses. Small tumblers. I hand one to Teddy, who turns it upside down before announcing, a childish smile breaking, 'I'm seventy-eight years old. What about you?'

I laugh as I learn the younger version of himself also played this game at the school canteen. We allow ourselves a short, tender pause. I open the pot to give the ragù a stir: 'We're eating tagliatelle con ragù alla Bolognese for dinner.'

Teddy pours us wine, a ripe cherry colour, no further words.

'Ragù is simply a meat-based sauce. What makes it special is the type of meat you use, the simmering time you spare. Like most Italian dishes, it's versatile and made of simple but good-quality ingredients.' I defend my choice for tonight's menu.

Teddy nods, 'Go on.'

'The butchers in Bologna have their own, special ragù meat. They don't display their provenance, nor of what and how the mixture is made, but if you buy yours from them, then your ragù will always have that one, specific taste. Tonight we'll have to do with my Nonna's pancetta and fine beef from Lidl, though.'

'Tonight we're having Giulia's ragù,' Teddy corrects me as he approaches the hob. His pupils dilate with hunger and curiosity.

I smile back before I pick up the description of the ragù in front of us. Both our eyes are focused on the thickening sauce, the sticky texture and an explosive smell of summer rain pearling on woodland rocks envelop us. 'We do. My grandmother would have made hers with fennel instead of celery. Alessandro, my stepbrother, hates celery. He ate all his meals except Saturday lunches with his mother, yet the rest of us had fennel in our ragù all year long.' I struggle to hide resentment in my voice.

Teddy brushes my forearm. 'Well, I hate fennel. Can I taste this famous ragù now?'

I hand him a spoon and my eyes lock with Teddy's lips. He breaks into a smile, so I continue. 'Ragù is something we'd have in the freezer all year long. But we also served it fresh for our traditional Saturday lunch. We came together, Alessandro and I played with construction toys made of wood underneath the table, Paolo caught up with *Il Manifesto* newspaper on his day off, my mother and grandmother worked away in the kitchen all morning. The ragù infused the entire house as they made fresh tagliatelle.' I can't turn down the rising volume in my voice, even though I worry this story excludes him from our future. I turn my eyes away. At least he is not a vegetarian, I tell myself in anticipation of Teddy's first weekend in Bologna.

Teddy bounces back, 'If Alessandro is your stepbrother, does that make Paolo your stepfather?'

I take my time to clear my voice. 'He isn't my biological father, correct. But he is the man who raised me. My nonna is his mother and she has always treated me like her grand-daughter. We're family, we have little care for bloodlines.'

His eyes have left me as he plays with the piece of string I used to tie bay leaves to the pot's handle. We had a bay tree back home, its branches were perfectly cut in a round shape, the large terracotta pot moored in the corner of our balcony for seasoning and hiding our routine from the neigh-bours' curious looks. My nerves fizzle inside. *Don't play with your food, Giulia.* Marija's voice hits me with her tales of drought and dry ground, until Teddy brings me back to London, the green grass and the longing river Thames, both a fence and a pathway across the metropolis.

He looks up and meets my eyes, his fingers still fiddling. 'I was also raised by a different man than my father. My real name is Theodore Junior, after my paternal grandfather, the most respected man in the family, apparently.' Teddy's voice follows a rhythm I am not accustomed to yet, his usual calm beat coupled with a low tone at the end of his sentences, *apparently*. 'One night, my father went out to meet his mates at the pub, he said.' *He said.* 'He never came back and my mother started to call me Teddy.' *Teddy*.

'Madonna.' I softly close the drawer before me, a pack of tagliatelle pasta in my hands nonetheless. It had never crossed my mind that Teddy might be a nickname. How did I not realise this before? Theodore. My boyfriend is called Theodore and I did not notice. I reach for his hand, our fingers tighten, 'I like it.' He raises his eyebrows. 'Theodore is a beautiful name.'

He smiles. 'Am I getting so emotional that this pasta looks green?'

I snort, and my chin retreats inside my collarbone. 'They are green, fresh from the last parcel I received from home. Pasta verde, they are coloured with fresh spinach.' I bring a big pot of salty water to the boil, and Teddy's observant stare weighs over my shoulders. Silence as we process the truth we often easily forget; we were people of our own before we met. I search for a fact to rescue him from the memory he is not ready to share. I invite him home instead: 'Emilia Romagna is the region in Italy where people speak about food the most,' I say, slowly, so he can swing back into my intimate language. Teddy's right elbow pushes his body straight against the counter, his left hand reaches for the bottle of wine. Refill. 'The first time my grandmother gave me a prosciutto sandwich, my tongue stung with salt. But I knew why. She had explained to me that hams are salted and left to dry in the chilled air for weeks before they are sealed and sold. When a woman from Emilia Romagna is about to feed you, she'll tell you about the food itself first, its provenance and backstory. Always. For your food to taste good, you must care. My family taught me that.' I tip the pasta into the boiling water. 'Bologna, the region's capital, is nicknamed *La Grassa*, after the abundance of its food offerings and the richness of the recipes that transform them.' I cannot stop the rolling movement between both my eyes and lips, both moving upwards. 'We must go to Italy together for the twenty-fifth of April celebrations one day. We could even start early with a march to Il Pratello on the day Bologna was liberated, on the twenty-first of April.' I grow increasingly aware of the pace between my tongue, arms and legs. I force myself to pause, briefly. 'Bologna, which is known as the red city of Italy, is female after the women who inhabit and feed her streets and, if you ask me, because of her political heartbeat.' I ask Teddy to pass me the *thingy* next. His eyes meet mine with a question and I miss Claude in return. I reach for the colander myself. The tap runs cold water, I drain the long pasta, their tentacles floating like Paolo's trou-sers on the drying rack at the end of each week, Nonna's ragù simmering all day long on Friday, Saturday lunch and leftovers for the rainy days. I'm growing aware Teddy most likely doesn't know what April 25th stands for in Italy, that he simply did not like to ask, as he worried I would dismiss his ignorance. I return the pasta to the pot and incorporate some of the ragù sauce. I stir. 'Paolo is involved with the communist party and he'd bring me to these banquets where industrialists meet. We ate tagliatelle with meat ragù as they debated. You can imagine how excited I was, running around the benches, drawing mind maps of the world they were discussing. Each meal ended with a fruit, and I still love that about the banquets. It makes these men's soft hearts shine through their constant disagreement.' I am out of breath by the time I finish my account. Teddy, at the other end of the kitchen counter, hasn't moved. I continue, 'I find comfort in knowing that we were both raised by stepfathers. Even after all these years I still can't call Paolo *father*, I tried but it sounds as if I had wronged my mother, you know? I'm sorry I didn't ask about your name before.' His eyes are red and I invite him to sit at my table. 'Shall we eat our first ragù?'

The secret ingredient is time, Nonna reminded us with each generous portion, as Marija rolled her eyes with the defiance of those who have been on the run before. I feel regret. I should not have attempted a meal that requires slow cooking with the little time we have on our side. We need our own recipes with Teddy, a faster pasta, the carbs to push us through, a new family tradition for our generation. I stare at him anxiously as he takes a first mouthful of pasta, dripping ragù, and his shoulders relax against the back of his chair. He shakes his head in approval, a second mouthful for joy. I tell him that the ragù will be even better tomorrow, after a night sealed in the pot on the hob, the ingredients will have marinated longer. We make plans for tomorrow, ragù on toast for brunch before we go for a walk along the canal, cloudy breaths leading the way, a pint at the pub to end the day with the rugby game, a fireplace to warm our blood. The ragù will have settled then. We have another portion of pasta. Teddy tells me about his mother, who also adores a plate of pasta, simply with lemon or basil and cherry tomatoes. Perhaps he can cook something like this for me next time? Isabella works as a paralegal in Sydney but they live in the suburbs. We share childhood memories as we both had to sit in church on Sundays while our parents cursed the other six days. Teddy spills ragù on his shirt as he recounts his mother's obsession with astronomy and the nights they spent lying on their backs in their garden, the occasional mention of his father. His eyes escape through the window as he speaks and I let him wander the night sky for as long as he needs, another mouthful of tagliatelle to pick us up. All families have histories of their own, and not all past stories build foundations for the present. The future is ours, I want to believe.

'Would you like a tangerine for dessert?' I squeeze Theodore's hand as I stand up and move towards the kitchen counter, dirty plates in my hands. I drop them in the sink and sigh with relief. Time is our remedy.

Stretching Winter

1

12 December 2019. The air is moist and heavy and the sky overcast. As Claude walks out of her flat, towards the local primary school that has been converted into a polling station for the day, she draws on all her strength just to put one foot in front of the other. A few green and red leaflets hang in her neighbours' windows. The clocks are just about to chime seven and the streets are unbearably quiet. What she anticipated feeling remains unclear to Claude, but it sits somewhere between guilt from knowing she should have spoken up and protested, and the consuming feeling of powerlessness as she approaches the ballot box. Why is the ground not shaking and why is there no thunder in the sky? There will be hundreds of thousands of people heading towards polling stations today, returning to the repurposed school buildings for the space of fifteen minutes, and yet she

is alone when she arrives at her assigned station. Claude kneels down, throwing her bag on the floor; she cannot find her poll card. Her fingers grapple inside, increasing her feelings of anxiety, her heart causing her cheeks to redden – she feels apprehension today as if tomorrow will look different, yet she cannot unpick the fear that is growing within her. Anything and nothing feels possible, as she stands there, alone at the polling station.

Sophie follows in Claude's footsteps an hour later, at a busier polling station in north-west London. She sends a picture to Claude while she waits, worrying her friend might think she did not go to vote. Sophie rarely talks about politics because she is nervous to engage with the subject publicly. She knows that she has not cemented her opinion on most topics, and that most of the viewpoints she would formulate in a conversation would be retellings of what she had heard Allegra argue in the past. Sophie inherited a lot of political baggage from the dinner parties she grew up with, the bold and aggressive headlines of the newspapers that were delivered to her front door. She is envious of Giulia for speaking her mind so firmly and loudly, even more so in a language that is not her mother tongue. Sophie adores Claude's earnest side when it comes to the issues she believes in, for the environment, for equality, for fluidity. They exchange brief messages about today's elections until they drift back to the politics of their own lives. Tonight, Claude and Sophie will spend the evening together; the two of them only. Sophie suggested they go out to a restaurant, to catch up and to ignore the present dreadful shape of the world's map. The truth is that Sophie is scared of what might, or rather might not, happen today, and if the result is a bad one, then she would want to be with Claude. *The sadness we created for ourselves*, thought Claude when she agreed to meet. She found relief as she read through the menu online; imagining Sophie in her kitchen for their first proper reunion made her body tremble.

When Sophie arrives at the restaurant, she grabs her left wrist with her opposite hand, surprised by the coldness of her watch face against her palm. The streets of London are re-emerging from the first snow of the year. She pushes her hair back behind her ears. It has grown long, almost reaching the bottom of her shoulders. Claude enters her eyeline, a long black coat skimming her ankles as she crosses Frith Street.

'And obviously we must queue in honour of Giulia today,' announces Claude as she embraces the fragile bones she has missed dearly, the same cartilage that holds together this body that frightens her.

'They say it shouldn't be more than twenty minutes. Do you want a cigarette?'

Claude shakes her head. 'Are you anxious about tonight?'

'Silly, I know. It's been a long time but it's not like we have never shared a meal before.'

'I meant the election.' She smiles. Sophie is battling her

lighter, her nails scratching against the spark wheel. 'I'm happy we're doing this.'

They share the cigarette, the smell admittedly too tempting, their fingers brushing against the other, their cloudy breaths mingling. Claude looks stunning, sharp eyeliner, long fingers. When they are called inside, Sophie is catching Claude up on news of her business, her latest dreams for what make-up can mean and how it can be produced, and the latest shows they have secured for the Spring season. She owns her career. Sophie's sentences gush between her excitement and her desire not to let Claude ask the questions she does not want to answer.

They expected to be seated at the bar, where friendships dine while restaurant managers safeguard their rare tables for the dating pairs. Tonight is different, however, as the waiter shows them a small corner table for two, both warm and intimate. They hand him their coats and order red wine. When the bottle arrives, they are focused on the other and pay no attention to the cork being removed; not even the popping noise makes their eyes slide away. Sophie cries with laughter when Claude tells her about the day she created her dating profile as she baked a lemon pie; 'Very Julia Child of you,' she concludes, as her laughter simmers down and leaves room for a tight and peaceful smile. There is a moment of seriousness once Claude has confessed she is going to therapy, even though she kept her assignment to write a letter to Sophie quiet. They're not a good match, Claude and her therapist, who was assigned randomly by the system after she filled in an online form about what triggers she identifies and went through a long waiting list. 'She asks a lot of direct questions,' Claude explains, before adding that she is entitled to eight hours on the national health system. Sophie grabs her hand. She later shows her Dean's new girlfriend, or at least assumed partner as a consequence of the recent hours of stalking. Giulia has said, 'Certo. She is girlfriend material,' reports Sophie. Claude agrees. Nothing more will ever be said about Dean.

The restaurant is the size it takes to strike a profitable margin in Soho, enough chairs and thus mouths to feed, but a space that remains within the affordable remit of renting. The lighting is muted, candles burn by the wooden walls and ceiling; sparks of golden yellow shine against the dark brown colour of the tables. They offer a range of sharing plates, 'to make the most of the convivial art of eating,' explains the waiter. Claude rolls her eyes. This setting feeds into the uncertainty of today, to eat your favourite dish fast so you make the most of it, to share and not to share so much either, to pretend it is about equality in public, with your mind running wild with the fear not enough will be spared for you. To find a compromise between the appetite of others and yours at the end of the day is an exhausting exercise, they both agree upon this once the waiter has slipped away with their order.

The conversation has slowed down. Sophie suggests: 'Should we take a look at the exit polls?'

Claude looks back up to Sophie, her right hand making a gentle circle with her spoon against the thick porcelain plate: 'Would it matter?'

'They will be good pointers. But no, I don't think they're relevant to us right now.'

'What do you mean?'

'I don't think Boris or Corbyn will change the way I see you and I don't think politics are relevant to us.'

'Well, maybe they are, Sophie.' Claude stops, she refrains from adding a comment about the government that raised their mothers before them, about Sophie's mother. On the edge of an earlier decade, as the year 1989 was sealed as the warmest one on record and as rumours about the so-called greenhouse effect mounted, Allegra had witnessed the resignation of the longest-serving and only female UK prime minister to date. They are both silent for a short while, almost as if they remember, melancholia creeping in.

Allegra, the memory of her presence moving in a similar pattern to ocean currents, quiet and cold, regulates the atmosphere between both their lives. Sophie's eyes anchor into Claude's, set in stone from the attack, gearing up to fire back. Claude closes her eyes before she continues, 'The fact you think these politics don't apply to us is part of the problem. Our problem.'

Sophie's neck straightens, her hair falling. 'Are you insinuating that I'm a coward?'

Claude stares back at Sophie: 'I think that you hide, and therefore I do too.' *The sadness we created for ourselves*, Claude whispers, only to herself this time.

'If you're so aware about yourself, about me,' Sophie's voice breaks, 'about us.' She pauses briefly before she picks up words again, composed this time. 'Have you considered that you might be the one who failed to give me the confidence to be myself?' Sophie reaches for the bottle of water. She fills her empty wine glass. 'Do you want to know what I think? I think that you hide behind your constant refusal to label anything. Pull out the political card if you want, but as far as I'm concerned, you're the one who is trying to define us behind a set of rules. Your set of rules.'

Sophie pushes away the leftover food from her plate. Claude scans the room, suddenly aware they are dining in one of the few restaurants that does not play a loud soundtrack in the background.

'What set of rules are you talking about?' Claude asks with a low voice.

Sophie takes a sip of water, clinking her glass against her plate. 'The house in Provence, almond and strawberry tarts, counting in French, everything that makes who we are.' Another silence. 'What we should call ourselves.'

Rather than the words, the defiant glow in Sophie's eyes is what brings Claude's blood to the boil. This look, gunshot-like, piercing through her body, is one she has known well since their early days. The same look as when Sophie called out to teachers from the classroom's last row to attract attention away from their classmates, when she entered any party during their university years, when she introduced Allegra's memorial. Shooting eyes, a desire to disarm any potential conversations, destructive stare.

A rapid shiver, then Claude murmurs: 'I simply cannot afford not to know what we are.'

Trembling lips, Sophie turns her eyes away. *You're the one who is leaving,* hangs between them, another shiver swirls.

Leftover rice sticks together into small, cold balls at the bottom of a dish. Claude recomposes herself, moving forward from the back of her chair towards the table: 'All is said for tonight. Let's get the bill.'

Sophie brings her glass back down on the table, clinking it once again against her plate. 'You should probably know that I voted Lib Dem this morning.'

'Please, enough now. You're acting like you're drunk'

'The last time I was, it didn't stop you from fucking me.' Sophie gazes at Claude.

'That's it. I'm going.' Claude pushes her chair backwards but Sophie grabs her hand. 'Can I come with you?'

'Not tonight, Sophie.'

Claude raises a hand, desperate to bring the waiter's attention towards them this time. She continues to draw circles against her empty, oily plate as her eyes refuse to look at Sophie. It is a political act to love, to love despite our primitive instinct to protect ourselves. The noise from the metal spoon against the porcelain has grown louder and Sophie excuses herself as she walks in the direction of the bathroom.

When she reaches the top of the stairs on her return, she finds Claude is standing by the door, wrapped in a scarf, sunny yellow earrings shining through. Sophie's phone vibrates, the screen lighting up between them as she lets Claude know her cab has arrived, shyly, aware of how long it has taken her to resurface, surprised that Claude waited.

Claude kisses her tenderly on the cheek before adding, 'I don't sleep with centrists, you know that. Get some rest, Soph.'

She closes the door behind Sophie and walks towards Oxford Circus Tube station, taking the long way around Soho, detouring through the narrow streets and hidden mews, grasping faint snippets of conversation from the crowds outside the pubs, gasping the ambient air. When she looks at her phone again, she finds a message from Giulia:

Get your French passport sorted ASAP!!!!!

She wishes she could laugh at Giulia's dramatic message, even more so at the inappropriate photo of the future prime minister that accompanies it. On any other night, she most likely would have engaged in a quick search for a more ludicrous photograph. Tonight she is exhausted. She returns her phone to her bag, letting the escalators take the responsibility of carrying her numb legs downwards, towards the Victoria Line, welcomed by a crowd of commuters and an embracing smell of cold beer.

The hangover Claude and Sophie experience the next day is bitter, reminiscent of the morning after the Brexit referendum but without Giulia this time, a first taste of what this island they call home could become, in the shape of a country and in the form of their friendship. Time passes, while they do not talk but contemplate what the other might be doing, scrolling through their respective timelines, in search for a good enough article, photo, or even an event to forward, as a peaceful handshake. Giulia wakes up on the other side of the Thames, early enough to find the news is the sole notification on her screen:

**BORIS JOHNSON BECOMES
THE 55TH PRIME MINISTER
OF THE UNITED KINGDOM.**

She throws the blanket away and before she can think further, she is wearing her running tights and tightening her smart-watch onto her left wrist. Today it is Giulia's turn to race with the clocks before they reach 7 a.m., conquering the empty streets of London. She slides into her sneakers, sets her watch to tracking mode, and slams the door behind her. Before she turns around the first intersection, a smile is lighting up her face. She feels liberated and empowered, in control of her body, which is carrying her forward through this city. If she can run fast enough, they will not be able to catch her and she will not have to leave. A cat is sleeping between a curtain and a windowpane, the barista at the local coffee shop opens the front door, letting the smell of warm butter come out in clouds as Giulia inhales deeply, as she pushes her pace faster. She always follows the same route, because it is the only way for her to track her speed, and because she likes to record time passing, the plants growing in the alleys, the bins out on Wednesday mornings, the postman on Kingsley Street, and then the family getting into their car on Wontner Road. There are three loops to Giulia's running route, depending on how long she decides to run that day. On 13 December 2019, she is following the longest circuit and she is not listening to any podcasts, her brain calibrating, her muscles pulsing with blood, rushing through her cells. She turns right at the library because today she wants to run uphill. This is her favourite: her knees working hard, pushing through, her breathing adapting to her pace, swear words flooding her brain when it gets harder not to stop, but she continues. Once she reaches the top, she bursts into the widest smile, extreme joy, cathartic, almost. She has never confessed she does this to anyone — that she runs up a hill and then laughs with herself, launching her body downhill, arms open, inhaling the city — because this is a coping mechanism of her own. Soon she will need to register her passport and provide her addresses for the last three years, and anything else the government requires in order to decide if she can be granted the right to stay and to continue to pay taxes in this country. *Indefinite right to remain*. This sharing will be a mandatory condition of her rights to run through London and the United Kingdom. But today her running trail is hers, her building tool for her own history with the country she inhabits. Giulia's personal map on which she asserts her form of belonging, which helps her to discover new corners and come to terms with fears and doubts as her steps set the tempo. This is her indefinite right to remain.

On the thirteenth day of December 2019, Claude, Giulia and Sophie's bodies ache.

2

The light pollution is reaching its apex in London as the sun goes down on 21 December. The end-of-year celebrations are fast approaching and the country is angry about the size of the Christmas tree in Trafalgar Square, small and uneventful, in comparison to the year they are drawing to a close.

The next day opens with Claude's loud footsteps echoing around the Walthamstow flat, she is speaking to herself, making lists as she goes back and forth between the rooms, her mind buzzing from picking what is essential and what is not.

Claude stops, cheeks red and fingers trembling: 'Will you take good care of my flat, then?'

'It will be an honour,' replies Sophie, a defiant smile on display as she rests her feet on top of the coffee table, her eyes engrossed in a thin paperback in front of her.

Claude responds with her hands rushing towards the sky as she runs back to the bedroom, where she is still sorting out her clothes, making space for Sophie's wardrobe. She has already written sticky notes about how frequently each plant needs watering, where to kick the washing machine to restart the drum when the door won't unlock, about the heating and what is the most ecological temperature and schedule.

All there is left to do is to make room for Sophie and to step outside.

Sophie sold the house in Hampstead. Allegra's perfume remained strong, impossible to chase away, and, like the perfume, the house turned bittersweet, as it happens when one shares a space with an inhabitant who is never home. She grew surprised at how frustrated one can be towards objects that do not seem to have a purpose nor a regular user, as if they were only there to steal space away from her. She spent long evenings staring at china vases and sculptures in silence, the clocks ticking harshly, *tic tac tic tac tic tac*. Sophie grew angrier at the house with each new day. So she decided to sell in order to halt her resentment towards the memory of her mother. Her father has not set foot in the UK for a long time, living another life with his family in the States as he has done for as long as she can remember. It would have ceased Allegra's pact with life to divorce – the reputation she had created for herself, at least – so he kept his new relationship discreet until the day she died. Sophie was briefed on the morning preceding her first day at school, and since that day she has wondered what their house looks like. Does it hide behind a tall fence made of trees? Mark calls Sophie for the occasions he defines as worth his time; he sent flowers the day she hosted her first showcase. He called her *daughter* when he learnt about the broken engagement, from Allegra, who was fuming. Allegra argued that Dean was a golden ticket, a perfectly fine man for her to create what she wanted for herself on the side. Mark is the one who comforted Sophie, agreeing that a photogenic marriage is a trap. He had met Allegra through the lens of his camera, as she pinned the dresses of the models he photographed, falling both in and out of love rapidly. For the first time in Sophie's life, her father confessed that he was proud of her, for standing up for herself. Down a crackling phone line, he chose to finally share precious and missing pieces of his life with Sophie, about his partner Ruth, how they met and how they lived. Sophie is slowly building her relationship with her father now, exchanging shy text messages, mainly visual as they do not have a shared, familiar vocabulary yet. She has accepted that if they use words, she grows disappointed at this man who ignores the incidents that made the woman she has become.

As she turns the next page of the modern classic paperback she is reading, the narrator describes one of the protagonists as someone who can forgive but not forget. Sophie sighs at the cliché of this statement, which jars with the rest of the book, and with her own experience. She looks up, her eyes following Claude as she sweeps rapidly through chests of drawers and clunky wardrobe doors that do not close anymore. Her mouth warms up to the idea of debating this out loud; they never talked about the episode at the restaurant again. She wants to be reassured that she is not the only one who cannot forgive if she is not able to forget the wrong in the first instance. One cannot forgive and own a truthful and objective memory of what caused the act that needs to be forgiven, or does Claude remember each one of their disagreements and hurtful silences? Or perhaps more than just forgetting, it is also about accommodating a memory of the harm as a necessity for forgiveness. If she has found herself in this flat today, it can only be because they have both decided to build their own version of the past that unites them in the present. They have silently agreed to be biased, she concludes, and thus Sophie decides against sharing the line with Claude in the end. She does not want to compare their subjective memories of what holds and scars their relationship together. Instead, Sophie brings the book back up to cover her face and reads the passage again, this time continuing past the sentence, content to disagree.

It was Sophie who suggested to Claude that she could move into her flat while she is in Rome, 'so the walls won't turn into mould,' she first explained. Claude acknowledged in return that it grows humid in the flat in winter. Sophie admitted that she needed somewhere to pause time, a familiar set of four walls, so she could decide what to do next. She closed the conversation by proposing a price for rent and Claude responded that she liked the idea of moving ahead while someone continued to switch the light on and off in her London home.

With the year approaching the finishing line, they have not spoken as much. They have not seen as much of Giulia either, who is flourishing: busy with work and Teddy. A year ends and the next day another one will bring a new lot of issues. Claude will be going back to school, Sophie will learn to live on her own, and Giulia will invite Teddy to be part of the memories in the making they are building.

Claude's phone rings but she does not pick up the call. She walks towards Sophie instead, and hugs her friend tightly. They take the time they need to shed quiet tears. Sophie drops a kiss on Claude's forehead, 'Go on now, I hear the Italians have an appetite.' They both smile and Claude closes the door gently behind her. Downstairs, Giulia is waiting for her in her tiny orange car, playful smile on. She has made a playlist for the journey to the airport. 'You need a good soundtrack to launch your next chapter,' she announces. They arrive at the airport faster than Claude had hoped they would. She turns her head towards her friend and is hit by the memory of Giulia, wide curls, minidress, dancing in the middle of a room full of strangers, as if no one else existed. She wants to remember her friend this way as she lands in Rome by herself.

Giulia gently looks back at Claude. 'Go on now, *kiss and fly*, as my mother would have said.'

Claude nods, one hand on the door handle: 'I'm going to miss you so much. Take care of Sophie, OK?'

'And you take care of yourself, Claude.'

Claude slams the car door behind her.

Sophie

I avoided the kitchen for days. I had little appetite and ordered the occasional takeaway sushi meal to take me through the hours. The reassuring *Place This Order Again* button, the steady rhythm of watering Claude's plants and herbs and emptying the washing machine brought a circularity to my otherwise spiralling thoughts. The boredom as a consequence of my non-existent domestic life, the exhaustion that stole away my former passion for my career.

The practice of quick calm cooking, I read in the table of contents. Beautiful photographs, wide white frames and passata drops, yellow stains from the turmeric powder Claude adores, oily fingerprints guide me through the cookbook. *A Modern Way to Cook* is the title, the recipes are organised in timeframes, 'in the time it takes to set the table'; 'ready in twenty'; 'on the table in half an hour'. The chapters unravel until we return to the early hours, 'super-fast breakfasts'. I can relate to this short-paced rhythm of time more than the one of meals and seasons. It had never occurred to me that Claude owned cookbooks. The most confident home cook I know, the one who always leads us to her table, needs such a tool, I realise. I continue to flick through the pages, my stomach grumbling for the first time since summer abandoned the city, hungry to know more about what Anna Jones cooks for herself. She details who she tried a recipe with for the first time, which season each flavour blossoms in; she gives advice about substitutes, preserving and temperatures. Her recipes open up like selfless acts of love. There is a history behind the ingredients and there are stories before the meals.

Puy lentils, the green lentils that are harvested in the French region of Le Puy, Claude once taught me, as she held a wide jar of mud-like green pearls in her hands with pride. I find myself back in the yellow kitchen, the heavy cookbook dragging at the end of my arms. I walk towards the same container of pulses, one Claude filled up before she left for Rome, ready to make Anna Jones' 'favourite lentils with roast tomatoes and horseradish'. Sudden memories: the ready-made horseradish sauce Allegra used to dig out from the cupboard to pair with Dean's roast beef for Sunday lunches. The thick spread stored in a glass jar with an elegant black label ribboned around it, the one I never tried before. I manoeuvre, the oven preheats and the kitchen finally warms up. I switch on the radio but it fails to play music. December, the sun makes rare appearances, the Christmas songs on repeat freeze my blood. I reach for my phone instead. I need voices to distract myself from the sound of the pots and wooden spoons, the slamming noise of the oven door, their music ear-splitting since there is no one else to share a meal with. I am alone. I do not miss Dean. I miss the sense of purpose of building a family, my revenge for a lonely childhood. I am cooking myself a solo supper for the first time. In a casserole, I put together the Puy lentils, a whole tomato, an unpeeled garlic clove and a few thyme leaves. I bring the water to the boil, leave the pot to simmer and I press play on my phone's touchscreen. *Olive, Again.* The audiobook begins. The lentils will simmer for the next half hour, so in the meantime I roast the tomatoes. I cut them into halves before placing them cut-side-up on a baking tray, together with salt, pepper and the zest of a lemon. I follow the recipe meticulously. I skip the breadcrumbs. *I do not have a clue who I have been. Truthfully, I do not understand a thing,* Kimberley Farr's voice reads in the background. I surprise myself as I snort, the echo follows closely, 'Neither do I, Olive. Neither do I.'

I stir the lentils gently until the water has evaporated. I sharply clang the wooden spoon against the edge of the casserole. I forget to set a timer, my thoughts adrift. I cannot remember the last time I visited the Monument. I miss the stairs, even more so since the flat on Fleeming Road is organised around one, narrow corridor. I mutter as I go, small encouragements to myself. I am alone in the kitchen. There is little else to do as the food cooks, the tomatoes roast in the oven, causing their skin to split. The lentils simmer softly. I read the instructions again to make sure I haven't missed any crucial steps. I start grating the horseradish to make the sauce. I will switch the cottage cheese with crème fraîche, our favourite kind of dairy in the yellow kitchen. Some rules are made to last. I mix the sauce and set it aside. I returned to the hospital for monitoring earlier this month, my results still unclear, like the blood that fails to bleed and the scarring that crosses my uterus. The excuse, *stressful life events such as grief can delay menstruation cycles.* My cycles derailed before Allegra's passing. The water from the casserole has evaporated. Was I already grieving my mother before she died? I set the lentils aside and scoop out the tomato and garlic. I turn them into a paste with the help of a fork, and I smile. I smile as I push through the vegetables, the smell of garlic filling the room, the tomatoes juicing with life as they release small pips of sunshine. Their hard skin has broken. Allegra's lips would have tightened to a firm close; she did not like anything that might stain or smells that might last. Do we always grieve our mothers? The expectations we build, the irrevocable duty we have towards each other – *the mother and daughter bond* – life getting in the way, the unavoidable failure we will experience. The only meal I ever saw Allegra cook is a roast. She started early on Sunday mornings, the meat changing alongside the butcher's prices and whims, always selecting the most tender one. Allegra often reminded me that the cause of the animal's death influences the taste of the meat. I disagreed. We argued about the difference between cause and effect. Not the cause as such, not the instant of death only, but the animal's state of mind as death struck, the lingering effect of a lifetime, modifies the texture of the meat, is what I believe. The nerves become harder to chew as anxiety rises. I stir the paste together with the lentils and add a drizzle of olive oil and red wine vinegar to the mixture, just as the recipe instructs me to do. I top up the lentils with the tomatoes and horse-radish sauce and I sit at the dinner table. I do not drink tonight. I am doing battle. There is nobody to stage a dinner for. I will eat.

The wooden table where Claude, Giulia and I have assigned seats, a silent agreement between us, wobbles. One mouthful after another, I pace along with my fear of swallowing, the repulsive Adam's apple sliding up and down my throat in the same nonchalant, automated way the elevators operate back in the office. The building I rent, the arch of the busi-ness I built and still run, the employees who rely on me increasingly as each month ends. Loud days, fraught evenings and insomnia. I spike the roasted tomatoes so their juice streams through the lentils, their liquid slows down as it meets the thick horseradish sauce. I play with flavours I created for myself. I drift back to the memory of Allegra in her kitchen, the walls perfectly white, the cupboards that seal pans, pots and plates to a soft close. I found food in our fridge at all times. Allegra, the quiet strength that rules my world, the tender scars she bequeathed me. I scrape the bottom of my bowl. The scratching noise echoes with my teeth which will grind later tonight. People used to say we have the same jawline, mother and daughter. *I do not have a clue who I have been.* I now realise that it was me and the fear of failing the expectations I set for myself that made me feel ugly. I want to be my own family. A functioning kind of family. I want a child. I don't know if Claude wants children. I don't need anyone to have children of my own. *Single mothering*, I murmur, the sound of my voice bouncing back against the walls. The colour yellow stands for the late rising sun. Allegra paved the way first, the women I surrender myself to light up this path. I can break away from the familiarity I have sheltered within until now.

Tonight I ate a supper for one, composed of French-grown lentils, explosive San Marzano tomatoes and a twisted horse-radish sauce, the story of the first meal I cooked for myself. Some rules are made to be broken.

The Finale

The abortion law came into effect in Ireland, Patti Smith played at the Roundhouse in London, an asteroid brushed the earth, Theresa May resigned and people marched. Brexit is going ahead. Extinction Rebellion manifested in pockets of resistance: bodies glued to trucks, pupils studying for their final exams on Waterloo Bridge. The Hong Kong protests sparked and continue. Toni Morrison died. The rainforest was set on fire. Astronauts Christina Koch and Jessica Meir completed the first spacewalk with an all-female crew. The diaries now read *December 2019*, and despite everything, Boris Johnson was elected prime minister with a reported share of 43.6 per cent of votes, even though who is sharing what remains unclear. There are rumours mounting about a virus but most of us do not feel concerned or foresee, rolling into the 20s, that it will soon swipe lives away, far away and near home, redefining where domesticity roots and blossoms, and that we will not have the tools to count or bury the dead.

* * *

Sophie exits Oxford Circus Tube station towards the end of the afternoon, before the crowd arrives to watch the London fireworks, welcomed by a mild winter day and the bright lights, a peculiar shade from the streets built around shopping vitrines. She mechanically turns right on Hanover Street, attracted by the imperial door that upholds the golden letters, *Vogue House*, headquarters of the Condé Nast business. This monumental door Allegra once pushed. If you look inside, your eyes will be met by the personalities who made this past year's front covers for *Vogue*, *Vanity Fair*, *GQ* and other lenses of the Nast empire in the UK and around the globe. Lush bodies sculpting time and echoing major events through the glossy means of fashion, culminating with Phoebe Waller-Bridge, golden dress and daring look, game on for the *Vogue* December 2019 issue. 'I always want to be dangerous', the front page quotes her as saying. Sophie buttons up her coat, her eyes tightening as she pictures the framed *Vogue* January 1990 cover that once hung in the family Hampstead home's entrance hall. Allegra's eyes watered each time she recounted the story of Cindy Crawford, Naomi Campbell, Tatjana Patitz, Christy Turlington and Linda Evangelista walking, wild smiles and explosive energy on display, through New York City's meatpacking district, Giorgio di Sant' Angelo bodysuits tucked into their Levi's. On the other side of the 80s, with push-up bras, no fuss about their hair, very little make-up, they announced the supermodel era, the years Allegra thrived. Sophie turns left onto New Bond Street, hit by the loud music that emanates from the pink striped walls of the flagship Victoria Secret store, a queue forming round the corner, giggling teenagers running out. She smiles as she remembers. New Bond Street stages a row of luxurious cages – Mulberry, Chloé, Hermès, Burberry, Louis Vuitton, Chanel, Dior – white lighting picking out velvet and glittery outfits under the spotlight. The mannequins are made of wood or grey fibreglass plastic. Sophie dreams of painting their expressionless faces, a mirror of this New Year's Eve, with vivid green colouring, shades of nudes, raspberry lipstick, peach blush, even purple glitter. Giulia had invited her to Italy; Claude said she wanted to begin 2020 on her own, as she set the ground for her new life in Rome. Nick invited Sophie to a party but she has still not responded. First she will take a walk, enveloped in her navy fur coat, Allegra's perfume more present than it ever was. The last evening of the year was her mother's favourite, and for as long as she can remember counting those last ten seconds to midnight out loud, there has been a party hosted at their home in Hampstead. Studio 54, Années Yéyé, the Astoria Club, are the themes Sophie remembers most vividly. Each night was kicked off by Allegra's entrance down the stairs, everyone's gaze turning towards the ornate vision of her mother, a little sprinkle of nude eyeshadow and wearing a statement necklace, Sophie's eyes screening the room, her intake of breath as the attendees were wowed.

Sophie continues on, until New Bond Street becomes Old Bond Street, where the toothless mannequins make way for nailless hands, advertising rings from Cartier, Tiffany & Co. and Boucheron. Sophie shivers as the winter sun is now at its lowest, the thick light turning into a polar blue. She walks faster, blinkers on, until she hits the bustling Piccadilly. Her smile broadens as soon as she sets foot on this gigantic artery of London, where the Christmas lights are still up, music playing on the streets. Allegra loved Piccadilly, home of the Royal Academy of Arts, her favourite building and courtyard in terms of architecture. She had confessed to Sophie that throughout springtime she had lunch on the grass in Green Park once a week, walking through New and Old Bond streets, picking up a sandwich at the Grand Café along the way. Allegra smiled when she told Sophie this. Abruptly, for the first time, Sophie had glimpsed what her mother might have looked like as a child, this clever and fast-thinking girl, who had bigger ideas than she had confidence to break the rules. No later than ten days after the engagement happened, they had met at the Wolseley on Piccadilly with Dean's parents – at Allegra's favourite table – to celebrate while the appetisers were served, and to plan as the meal developed into further courses. Sophie's eyes water with joy when she thinks back to this lunch. The engagement was broken but this meal is one Allegra and Sophie had hosted together, mother eyeing her daughter, approving and celebrating. Sophie pushes through the door of the square and imposing building made of Portland stone. She is soon welcomed by the warmth of the polished walls inside, softened with blue York stones, emphasised by the white-and-black marble flooring. The wide room is loud, chatter from tables featuring European-style dining echoing against the red lacquer columns. Everyone who walks into this restaurant feels entitled to the abundance of food, alcohol trays wheeled through the room, pyramids of treats from the tea parties, all pointing towards the chandeliers that hang from the ceiling.

Sophie settles at the bar and orders a dry Martini with two olives. She toasts her mother, matching pearl earrings and necklace, creamy hands twisted together, *when a woman smiles, then her dress should smile too*, she can hear Allegra authoritatively quoting Madeleine Vionnet.

'Happy New Year, Allegra,' Sophie whispers before the first sip.

★ ★ ★

Seven nights have passed since Giulia walked through the front door of her family home in Bologna, one hand tightly holding onto Teddy's. She fought with Paolo and her step-brother throughout the week leading up to their arrival, relentlessly refusing their offer to drive to the airport to pick them up. She wanted Teddy to enter the city via the railway. She wanted to walk through the door with Teddy as her sole companion. Marija sealed the vigorous battle, taking a stand for her daughter to choose the route for her home-coming.

Since the second their long-anticipated arrival fell into the sphere of the past, time has blurred into an infusion of conversations, nods and laughs. Paolo and his son Alessandro marched Teddy to the bar on Christmas morning, while Giulia stayed home with her Nonna and mother. She had dreamt of introducing her partner to them – she craved their approval – but she missed spending time with the two figures that most influenced her womanhood. She missed the feelings of humility, wholesomeness and safety that inhabit a room where only familiar pronouns are in use. They started pottering around the kitchen early in the morning, the radio on in the background, Marija's hips dancing between cupboards and hobs, giving more vegetables to peel and slice to Nonna, who was settled at the table. Her body leaning against the door frame, Giulia stayed still, smiling, her senses lightened among the familiar energy of her women. Then she decisively walked to the hob, grabbed the wooden spoon and began to stir the beef ragù, chin high, eyes meeting her mother's look as she grabbed the salt. Marija smiled at her daughter: 'Promiješaj, Giulia, promiješaj is how you say "stir, Giulia, stir" in Croatian.' Giulia nodded, her focus going back to the bubbling sauce, her lips tightening under the pressure of her teeth wanting to bloom into a smile. Nonna approached the sink with a slight limp in her gait, not making a sound, to wash more potatoes. Giulia is home.

It hurt Giulia when Teddy's lips frowned at the corners, showing disdain as they first walked through the living room, where they found the worn-out leather sofa, the shelves full of random ornaments and dusty picture frames. The house has nothing in common with their minimalist London apartments, appearing foreign and old-fashioned, enclosing history from within. These lips she often burns to kiss have rejected where she comes from. Her head turned away in a rush to forget the moment she had noted, fearful she might never feel warmth when they kiss again. This slow-burning jittering feeling lasted for the first few days of their stay in Bologna, Giulia's eyes and senses scrutinising Teddy's gestures as he navigated his way through her Italy. Marija relentlessly told her daughter to be patient, each evening as they kissed goodnight, until she was comforted by Giulia's face brightening up, her cheeks moving higher, her eyes widening; the body language in which she recognised her ardent and fierce girl.

A few hours after the men left for the bar, the door opened again, welcoming back Paolo's fast-paced but gentle voice, quickly followed by Teddy's fascinated eyes, full of a child-like admiring smile. At the sight of his innocent expression, Giulia's smile soared, taking pleasure to see her boyfriend, who had spent the two-hour flight on their way to Bologna engrossed in a language learning app, lost in a sea of Italian words. He was trying, and for once she was not the one lacking the words to pin down what her mind was feeling. It was his turn to feel publicly naked before her.

'Theodore Junior, ti vuoi mettere con me?' Giulia whispered as she joined Teddy, her eyes attentive, a different approach from the agitated fingers that had written the same sentence on exercise books years before, two boxes – '*yes*' or '*no*' – for her schoolmates to tick in response. She kissed Teddy.

On New Year's Eve they have dinner all together before Giulia and Teddy head out to the bar to meet her friends. She has reassured Teddy most of them will speak English – she is excited for him to meet her childhood friends, for him to grasp fragments of this side of her personality he knows so little about. She longs for him to see her laugh among them, little anchors of who she has become. Not even an hour after they had arrived home a week ago, Giulia had taken her violin out from its case, Teddy's eyes doubling in size from the surprise, Marija clapping her hands with excitement and Paolo putting away his newspaper so they could sit back on the sofa, all together as a family. She had omitted to tell Teddy that the violin is an instrument she plays on her own at night and to her family when she is home in Bologna. In London and in their relationship, she grew shy about the strident melody she produces from her bow, about her *family lexicon*, as Natalia Ginzburg taught her during her first year at university. The sound of the violin is the music of Giulia's intimacy, one she is equally proud and shy of, just like the tones of her Italian mother tongue when she speaks in English, a trait of character she would like to be proud of, yet one that makes her voice feel somehow unworthy most of the time. Giulia found satisfaction in taking advantage of Teddy's lack of attention to detail, he who failed to notice the violin case she stored above their heads as they settled in the cramped plane. She stood calmly in front of her audience, the family that enabled her to believe she can do anything she puts her mind to. Her vision anchored into Teddy's stare, she began to play a soft version of 'Arrivederci Roma', soon met by Paolo's timid voice as he picked up the lyrics. Teddy's gaze blurred as tears fell down his cheeks, and Giulia's eyes remained fierce until she allowed herself a longer blink before the last chord.

Teddy is family now.

* * *

On the ninth day of January 2019, forty-nine refugees who had been stranded at sea for weeks, eyes from the so-called West turned away, were rescued and ships arrived in Malta after eight countries agreed to allow them within their borders, positioning their politics as one of openness, distracting the media's attention from how late their agreement was in the first place. Sea-Watch had rescued thirty-two people from an unsafe boat off the coast of Libya on 22 December 2018; Sea-Eye had rescued seventeen human lives on the following 29 December. All European Union countries had refused to offer safe harbour to the boats in any of their ports. Lives left at sea to drift. Souls drowning. Years passing. Dates merged and confused. History repeats itself. On 30 January 2019, Italian prime minister Giuseppe Conte announced that forty-seven migrants stranded aboard the *Sea-Watch 3* were allowed to disembark in Italy, from which point they would be directed to further borders. Asylum forms to be filled in for certainty, in which language still to be decided. The boat had been stranded in Sicilian waters for over a week by then, human bodies left with salty water only for hydration. Borders for fences. On 7 February 2019, flights in and out of Rome Ciampino airport were cancelled after three World War II bombs were discovered. The bombs weighed a combined 150 kilograms, including around 75 kilograms of gunpowder. It is estimated that 60 million Europeans became refugees during World War II. According to the United Nations, a million people had yet to find a place to settle by 1951. Since November 2019 and following the initiative of four bolognesi friends, tens of thousands have squeezed together like sardines in Italian city squares to denounce Matteo Salvini and his anti-immigrant rhetoric; the sparks of individual lives building a collective fire. On Friday 20 December 2019, 162 refugees, including at least

50 children, were rescued via the *Ocean Viking* ship just off the Libyan coast. They arrived in the southern Italian port of Taranto. Over a hundred human lives were fighting on a deflated rubber dinghy, their screams echoing with those who were holding onto a wooden boat.

How many lives will it take for 2020 to draw to a close? Time moves unequally, events slide from the front to the last newspaper pages, history is trapped in the world's echo chamber. Lives roll onwards, our blinkers on, pursuing happiness even after when most are denied the right to live a dignified life.

Claude

I landed in Rome Ciampino airport at midday. I had prepared my itinerary ahead of my journey and it appeared simple enough: a bus to the train station then a train to Termini and finally the metro, with only four stops to go. I scribbled the route on the back of an old envelope, the crafted rectangular brown paper that once held the birth certificate I had ordered online. This one sheet of paper, roughly photocopied from the archives, featured the exact hour and minute I saw the light and the word 'inconnu' for father before mother's full name: *Aëlle Gwenaela Thomas*. This one sheet of paper granted me one stamp that proved my French blood and secured my right to cross European borders on a whim. I felt disappointed at the straight line the plane followed from London to Rome, two cities aligned geographically, a simple and uneventful route to my next home, my eyes fixed on the small interactive map in front of me. Fear was crushing my stomach into small pieces. But then I caught sight of myself in the sparkly silver of the conveyor belt as I waited for my suitcase to be delivered, and they came back to me, rushing and shaky, unreliable and overwhelming, the memories of what led me to Rome. That very sense of self I had misplaced as I refused to make any change to my failing routine, as I grew afraid of who I might find. I am either angry or fearful and so then I am angrier at being fearful, which makes me fearful of myself. My fingers often feel numb in protest, refusing to hold a fork or to brush my hair back. I applied to this patisserie programme before I thought about the consequences, one day before the deadline, as if I was a thief running away from a stolen life: heart racing, legs starting to grow tired, and my brain ordering them to push through. Is this what Giulia meant when she said running made her feel empowered? Does Sophie feel this high from managing her own business? I handed in my notice at the café on the Monday after I received my acceptance letter to the traineeship. Sasha will now be running the place. I told Ciara I was leaving as I queued to board the plane. I thanked her for showing me that the world is bigger than I first thought with her enthusiasm for the outside world, the faith she has in slowing down the ticking clock humanity finds itself facing, against climate change and species extinction. Ciara was my wake-up call to the wild; my cold bath. I surrendered to Ciara and to the blissful taste she brought to my life at first, a rush of emotions and actions I was once too shy to sense, until I became so hungry, I refused to continue sharing. I found myself, my reflection, in the clunky and noisy machine processing my suitcase at Rome Ciampino airport, and I smiled at the sight of the Claude I captured: holding onto my passport tightly, short and sharp haircut, yellow earrings for framework.

The hardest goodbyes were for Maman. There was the administrative side of leaving her behind, organising care, a change of address, and finding a new emergency contact who is close enough geographically. Sophie. There were the silent and sleepy eyes Maman gave me for an answer as I explained where I was going, an untouched cake resting between us. I had baked the almond and strawberry tart Sophie adores the night before, my stomach burning with guilt. The next day, I woke up with regret at not having made a Betty Crocker zesty lemon cake. I considered not telling her at first. It was the nurse's advice: *She won't notice*, she explained. But I wanted to believe she cared and for her to care she needed knowledge in the first instance. My mother is my longest-lasting love, baths turning cold between us. She did not intend to get pregnant, she refused to push when she went into labour, and then she surrendered to the shelter of her own mind. I envied my mother for years; Maman who lives with her own thoughts, who follows her own pace. Never have I seen her asleep nor have I seen her present, her gaze ever wandering, her sentences always short and affirmed. Her rare words are small stings, proof of her lack of interest in the rest of the world. Her sharp teeth had pushed into a homely smile as she read *The Call of the Wild* to me.

I remember. You can dismiss actions but the words that define them are made to stay. For my mother, there is no such thing as needing to be hungry at the same hour of the day as the rest of the members of an entire household. She eats or she doesn't eat and no one else factors in the rhythm of her bowels. Apart from me – I care because I don't want to be remembered as the failing daughter who did not ensure her mother has had a meal to eat, especially when I call myself a baker. Ugly sarcasm, a dry laugh to myself. I signed the paperwork, making sure she would have three meals served to her room every day, regardless of whether she eats them or not, and I moved on to feeding others whom I chose. I often look back because there is no forward movement without the memories that have shaped me in the first place, my coffee every morning flowing in memory of Maman's blood. I have learnt to live with the fact we will never walk at the same pace. Maman is ill and it does not have to mean that I am.

The year 2020 will strike me one hour before it will reach Sophie, leading the path through a new decade, a new set of hopes and fears. On the last day of December 2019 in Rome, low sky and a trickle of light coming through the few and shy clouds, I wake up early, swiftly approaching the hob, turning on the gas, listening to its whispering noise as the Moka pot works up to brewing caffeine. I sit back at the table, a cloud of warm coffee odour in front of me, my eyes following the ticking clock. Restless, I head out towards the market in Testaccio. I follow the longer route, listening to the scooters and trams as I walk, studying the buildings and the people who enter each one of them. I want to learn how they inhabit this city as I timidly take my first steps, poised to learn the skills we organically acquire through repeating the actions of our parents as children, but as an adult this time. In Rome, I am learning to walk, to speak a new language, to experience for the first time, once again. The vegetables and fruits have colours I had forgotten from the comfort of my yellow kitchen – I rarely cooked purple or orange, now I can see these shades clearly. I buy artichokes after my eyes were caught by their triumphant and baroque shape, longing for a meal that will result from the hard work of preparation, wanting to fill time with doing as opposed to thinking. I decide against a preparation alla Romana, instead I want to steam the vegetable as I assume my grand-mother would have done in Brittany, a tender dream of a childhood memory. I walk back to my apartment, high-ceilinged on the fifth floor of a large and heavy building, a shopping bag dragging on my shoulder, assured steps: I know the route this time around. I first slice off the base of the bulb, removing the stem. Then I begin to cut the outer leaves and trim the stinging top from the remaining leaves. I bring salted water to a boil, add the juice of a lemon and some pepper, place the artichoke upside down and cover. I leave it to steam for about thirty minutes but I do not leave the kitchen. Instead, I sit at the small table in the corner, one sticky hand holding my timer – *tic tac tic tac tic tac* – sucking the other thumb, as my gaze meets the chairs that are yet to host their first guests. This kitchen, painted in a dark olive green, has never heard the sound of a voice, apart from my occasional humming, four walls for an echo chamber. When the artichoke is ready, I bring it to the table and start tearing off each individual leaf with my fingers, sucking the meat, until I reach the cœur d'artichaut. It is then that I feel them, small, quiet tears, tracing my cheeks at a slow pace. I grab a piece of paper and I write to Sophie.

Dear Sophie,

I'm not accustomed to such fine weather in December. I even had ice cream yesterday, can you believe it? I have found my favourite gelato shop already. My favourite flavour is peach. You would love it. Do you remember the peach tart I once baked for us? It took us an entire Sunday while sipping wine. I like to think that all the baking we did together has led me here. It won't surprise you to read that I've created a new routine for myself. I've found a lovely apartment near the Fontana del Tritone. Not the Trevi fountain, which is slightly over the top if you want my honest opinion. From there, though, you can walk the beautiful stairs to the Terrazza del Pincio. I've been climbing up there in the evenings. I wish I had moved closer to the Mercato Testaccio now that I've seen the city with my own eyes. I love it there. The vegetables have colours and the fruits smell sweet. I order supplì first thing when I arrive and then I shop. I'm not sure you'd like the supplì – or at least the greasy marks they leave on my fingers and therefore my shirts. But they are delicious balls of rice and tomato sauce, coated in breadcrumbs and then fried. They are so gluey and warm. Anyhow I walk past

the Colosseum and the Circus Maximus to go food
shopping at the mercato – how decadent is that? Women
are incredibly stylish here. You'd love it. I'm not so far from
the Villa Borghese and I went for a run in the park there
once, making Giulia proud. She has been so helpful with
this move but I swear she is driving me nuts – now she
refuses to text me in English. She says I must learn. I'm
enjoying speaking a new language, although I struggle to
find the people I meet funny. Humour does not travel, I
suppose. Giulia says time is the secret ingredient. I saw the
lovely picture you posted of her, bright smile on the Heath.
It made me miss you girls and London dearly. How is my
little flat holding on? I hope the heating is working
properly. You would not believe it, but there are no heaters
in my flat here. Not that I need heating but somehow the
walls feel naked. I'm worried that I might get cold at night.
Are you sleeping? I count to 100 more often than I ever
have these days. I know it takes time for a new house to
smell like home but I fear it will never smell of your
perfume and that would be a first and I do not know if it
will ever be home then. Will you visit me one day? There
is a lovely hotel around the corner of my street where you
could stay, if you wanted to. I also have a sofa. And I have
a bedroom. I think I shall paint the walls soon – something
along the tones of peach. I miss you Sophie. How silly of
me to think I needed to move to a new country and hear
people talk in a language I do not quite understand and
live in a UNESCO-classified building to awaken my

heart. *Will you come visit me? You'd love it here. I'd love to have you here. As I said, there is a hotel around the corner, if you wanted. Do pack something other than your heels if you do come – we must walk through this city. We could paint the kitchen yellow together.*

Quatre-vingt-dix-huit. Quatre-vingt-dix-neuf. Cent. I know it is right to love now.

Clo xx

Acknowledgements

I owe the title of this book to the kitchen of Marguerite Duras.

I'm grateful to Johanna Clarke and Irene Olivo for listening and reading me the way they do; there would be no novel without them. Irene, Jo, thank you for your friendship. Thanks also to my early readers and friends: Ludovica Bevilacqua, Nicoletta Bucciarelli, Annalisa Eichholzer, Sara Langham and Valentina Paulmichl.

I owe a great debt of gratitude to my agent, Kirsty McLachlan, whose first email made me believe my voice could be heard. And I'm likewise indebted to my mentor, Alice Howe. I want to thank my editor, Clare Hey, who shared with me her love for cookbooks from day one, for her editorial notes.

My deepest gratitude goes to Ludo for making the last sentence of this novel meaningful. Ludo, thank you for our kitchen.

Author's Note

Dear Reader,

I am walking you down the stairs of a London flatshare. They are covered with a worn-out carpet, which used to be the colour of steel but is now stained with the prints of bike wheels, and splashes of coffee and wine. At the bottom, we find a kitchen with salmon-pink walls. On one side the shelves are cluttered with objects that current and old flatmates have collected over the years (cups – mostly chipped – bottles of liqueur, cafetières, coins from different countries, broken headphones and Oyster cards), on the opposite wall there are kitchen cupboards and a gas hob. There is a wooden table in the middle of the room – it wobbles because nobody can find the screwdriver anymore – and this is where I wrote most of my debut novel, *The Yellow Kitchen*. I don't live there anymore, but it was one of the many kitchens I have shared since moving to London, and I owe my voice to these kitchens.

I have threaded most of my friendships around cooking and eating. A committed introvert who interprets silence as a form of communication, I enjoy standing in front of the hob, swirling the contents of a saucepan with a wooden spoon and catching occasional sight of the person who is sitting behind me at the dining table. I hope they are snacking – a mixture of olives, some crisps, or I have splashed some olive oil and balsamic vinegar, with a pinch of salt and a sprinkle of oregano, into a bowl and sliced some bread for them – and I am listening. The frying chemistry of a soffritto is keeping me attentive and, there, I have noticed people open up. I love getting to meet someone while I cook for them, and I adore falling in love with them while we eat together.

I hope you have enjoyed reading *The Yellow Kitchen* and that it has been a good friend to you. There are days when I don't want to, or can't, cook for anyone other than myself. These are fine times too. Cooking is sensual and the kitchen is where I have discovered myself, where I have considered my cravings, explored the colours that inspire me to pair ingredients and worked out the smells that awaken my appetite; tasting and experiencing. Cooking conveys my lexicon and I could never have written my first novel in my second language if I hadn't learnt to trust my senses in the kitchen. I can't claim the vocabulary and grammar of a mother tongue in English, but I know what a teaspoon of miso does to my sardines on toast.

Whatever today is made of, I hope you can cook something nice for yourself or someone you love, so I'm leaving you with two recipes to make yours. The first one is for a versatile crab pasta dish that provides dinner for one or for a few, for new or old relationships, at a planned time or back from a night out, eaten at the table or straight from the pan. I have included a vegetarian variation made with asparagus and the measurements can be adjusted as you need.

The second recipe will please the sweet-toothed among us: a brioche tart recipe in which the fruit filling can be switched with the season's offering.

If your radio is as capricious as Claude's solar-powered one, you can listen to *The Yellow Kitchen*'s moody soundtrack here:

Bon appétit, and welcome to the kitchen space.

Margaux

Claude's Crab Pasta

'She is cooking crab pasta – it is tomatoey for Giulia and not too spicy for Sophie.'

For 4 people, you will need:

1 garlic clove, thinly chopped

1 bunch of flat parsley, thinly chopped

1 small chilli, thinly chopped

250g brown crab meat, undressed (tinned crab works well and makes it easier to adjust portion size from one to many)

1 gulp of dry white wine (optional)

400g canned tomatoes

400g rigatoni

Fresh basil to serve

In a pan, heat up some olive oil and cook the garlic, parsley and chilli over a medium heat. When fragrant, add the crab meat and the white wine (if using).

Once you cannot smell the alcohol anymore, add the tomatoes and lower the heat. Leave the sauce to simmer gently.

Meanwhile, bring a large pot of water to the boil. Add salt and cook the pasta according to packet instructions.

When the pasta is nearly cooked, lift it out of the water and transfer to the tomatoey sauce. Add a spoon of the cooking water, stir and leave the mixture to simmer for another minute.

Sprinkle basil on top, salt and pepper to taste, dive in.

Asparagus twist on a crab pasta:

In terms of ingredients, replace the crab meat with a bunch of asparagus (tougher bottom stems removed), roughly chopped. Start with boiling the asparagus until tender, set aside, and preserve the water to cook the pasta. Cook the pasta dish following the recipe above, but replacing the crab meat with the boiled asparagus.

The Yellow Kitchen's Strawberry and Almond Brioche Tart

For the dough:

1.5 tbsp dry yeast

2 tbsp milk, lukewarm

200g plain flour

2 eggs

½ tsp salt

15g icing sugar

90g butter, at room temperature

For the frangipane filling:

1 egg

60g butter, soft

50g brown caster sugar

80g ground almonds

600–800g strawberries, tops off and halved lengthwise (or see seasonal options below)

Start with making the brioche dough: pour the lukewarm milk into a small bowl, add the yeast, mix and leave to one side for approximately 10 minutes.

Meanwhile, on a work surface, make a volcano with the flour, salt, icing sugar and butter. Make a well in the middle of the volcano and add the warm yeast mixture and the eggs. Knead for at least 10 minutes, or until the dough comes together in a ball.

Place the dough inside a bowl. Cover with a damp tea towel and leave it to rest in a warm location for an hour and a half, or until the dough has doubled in size.

Preheat the oven to 180^C fan. Lightly press the dough down to remove any air bubbles. Line a baking tray with a sheet of baking paper and stretch the dough into a circle directly onto the tray.

Prepare the filling: whisk the egg, butter and sugar together. Add the ground almonds and continue to mix until combined. You're looking for a rich and thick consistency.

Spread the frangipane filling over the dough, then place the strawberries or fruits of your choice on top.

Bake for 25 minutes or until the dough looks golden and the frangipane has settled. Serve at room temperature or cold.

Sweet, seasonal variations:

This tart can be made with any fruits of your choice. I love it with apricots, halved and roasted with a sprig of rosemary beforehand. Apples, sliced; peaches, with a few spoons of crème fraîche; or frozen berries, if dried carefully so they don't release too much water when baking.